PUFFIN BOOKS

Gold Dust

Born and educated in Enfield, North London, Geraldine McCaughrean is the youngest of three children. After working as a secretary for Thames Television, she took a degree in Education at Christ Church College, Canterbury, though never taught. She worked at a London publishing house for some 10 years on such popular children's collections as *StoryTeller I & II* and *Little StoryTeller*.

She now works at home, in Berkshire and has published three children's novels, as well as compiling collections, and adapting many of the classics. *A Little Lower than the Angels* won the Whitbread Book of the Year children's novel award in 1987. She has also written adult books and radio plays.

Geraldine McCaughrean married her husband John in 1988 and has a daughter – Ailsa – born a year later.

Other books by Geraldine McCaughrean

A PACK OF LIES
A LITTLE LOWER THAN THE ANGELS

Gold Dust

Geraldine McCaughrean

PUFFIN BOOKS
in association with
OXFORD UNIVERSITY PRESS

PUFFIN BOOKS

Published by the Penguin Group
Penguin Books Ltd, 27 Wrights Lane, London W8 5TZ, England
Penguin Books USA Inc., 375 Hudson Street, New York, New York 10014, USA
Penguin Books Australia Ltd, Ringwood, Victoria, Australia
Penguin Books Canada Ltd, 10 Alcorn Avenue, Toronto, Ontario, Canada M4V 3B2
Penguin Books (NZ) Ltd, 182–190 Wairau Road, Auckland 10, New Zealand

Penguin Books Ltd, Registered Offices: Harmondsworth, Middlesex, England

First published by Oxford University Press 1993
Published in Puffin Books 1995
1 3 5 7 9 10 8 6 4 2

Made and printed in Great Britain by Clays Ltd, St Ives plc

Contents

1

THE HOLE

'What's he doing?' said Inez.

'Search me.'

'I mean, it shouldn't be allowed.'

'Maybe he wants to plant something. A bush or something. Mum would like that.'

'Dad wouldn't. You can't put a bush just anywhere. People would drive into it.'

Her brother Maro shrugged. So little happened on Main Street, Serra Vazia that a car driving into a bush might lend welcome excitement. But was that really why old Enoque Furtado was digging a hole in front of the town store?

Honorio, Enoque's brother, came along, and he too sank a pick into the dusty, packed earth. The dust blew down the street in little swirling eddies, disturbing a cat from the boardwalk outside the bank. Inez and Maro watched the men unseen, from the hammocks where they slept away the heat of midday.

'Maybe their dog buried something,' whispered Maro.

'Maybe *they* want to bury something.'

Their father, who ran the store, came out to stand on the boardwalk and smoke his single cigar of the day. A month ago his wife had allowed him two—one at siesta time and one after dinner. But business was bad, and times so hard that his ration had been cut back. The moment was a precious one in Mr da Souza's day.

Anxiety about the business had given way lately to a feeling of helpless despair. The unwanted goods on his shelves looked at him reproachfully, like unmarried daughters. Da Souza himself felt unwanted, left behind in this ghost town of a place, among the empty houses, with a wife and three children to support on the proceeds from a store where nobody shopped any more.

Bees were ambling to and fro among the crinum lilies Mrs da Souza had planted to brighten up the boardwalk. They had already been busy up among the poisonous nightshade on the football ground and wore pantaloons of golden pollen which exploded wastefully against the petals of the wilting lilies. Gold dust. Then da Souza saw the digging.

'Here! What do you think you're doing? Who asked you to dig up the place? My customers don't want to go tripping in a hole! People park there. People don't want to go parking down a hole!'

Enoque and Honorio rested on their pickaxes and wiped the sweat from under their collars. 'What customers?' said Honorio.

He had a point. Before the mountain failed, the town had heaved with humanity. Grandpa da Souza's store had thrived. But then the town had died—well, not died, perhaps, but contracted the painful, wasting disease which saw it shrink and shrink to its present sorry size.

The people had simply drifted away—left their wood houses and dry gardens and allotments straggled with dead bean plants, and disappeared. Where did they go? It was not clear. Was there really somewhere *better* outside Serra Vazia? Maro and Inez had no way of knowing.

'Well? What's it for, then? This hole. To bury something?' demanded Mr da Souza.

Enoque and Honorio looked at one another. Honorio put a finger in one ear. Enoque breathed in through his blocked sinuses with a noise like a broken gearbox. They were not going to tell the truth. Even Inez knew that much. It was the same when they wanted something from the store without paying cash: Honorio with his finger in one ear, Enoque snorting. 'Yeah. That's right. Bury a dog.'

'Yeah!' exclaimed Enoque enthusiastically. 'This dog ran out in front of the Jeep. No collar or nothing.'

'Bury a dead dog in front of my food store? Fetch in rats? Stink out the whole street? What are you? Sent by the Devil to curse me? What have I ever done to you that you come burying dogs in front of my shop!'

Maro looked at Inez and shook his head. The two Furtado brothers lived in a trailer on the edge of the football ground, arriving one long-forgotten day and forgetting ever to leave. The Jeep which had pulled the trailer into town currently stood half-way down Lisboa Avenue with no engine in it. So unless the dog had run headlong into the derelict Jeep, there was certainly no dead dog to bury in any hole.

On the walk back to school, Maro's imagination raced. Honorio and Enoque were obviously digging a tunnel under the shop to burgle it one night.

'Don't be ridiculous,' said his sister.

They were digging a bomb shelter against a nuclear war they had heard was coming.

'Don't be ridiculous,' said Inez. 'Why would Enoque and Honorio be the first to know?'

They were revolutionaries planning to overturn the President's car as it passed through Vazia.

'Don't be sillier than you were born,' said Inez with patient scorn. 'Enoque and Honorio are *garimpeiros*. They're gold-miners. It's all they know about. They don't have a brain between them to do anything else.'

'*Then they're mining for gold!*'

'Don't be ridic . . . ' But even Inez could not discount the obvious. Enoque and Honorio were digging for gold outside the shop.

Back at school that afternoon, Inez found her attention straying to the large figure decorating the classroom wall. It had been made by some previous year's children but left up by Senhora Ferretti as an encouragement to others. (There was a dinosaur, too, glaring out from between the book cupboard and the empty stationery locker.) The fat paper man on the wall had been daubed with glue then sprinkled with yellow sand from head to foot. His skirt was made from screws of gold foil sweet-wrappers. Beneath the collage the caption read, *El Dorado, King of the Manao*. As the glue decayed, more and more of the sand had trickled off to leave white patches: it seemed rather an undignified fate for the fabulous El Dorado. But perhaps it was no more than he deserved—if he ever existed, that is. Anyone who rolled himself naked daily in gold-dust and then pranced about, glittering and obese, probably deserved to end up commemorated in sand and sweet-papers.

Gold. A funny thing, really, for the world to place such value on, thought Inez vaguely. Something lying about in the ground. Why not something hard to come by? Something men had to climb up high for . . .

'Inez da Souza! Are you a member of this class or not?' Senhora Ferretti's operatic voice blared out, shaking the putty in the window frames.

'Yes, Senhora. I'm sorry, Senhora.'

'Well?'

'I—' Inez could feel her face burning.

'Well? *Have* you any ideas for our *Carnaval* theme this year?'

'Oh, I—well, no, but I . . . ' They had all been sent home to lunch with strict instructions to 'think of a theme'. But the silliness with Enoque and Honorio had put it clean out of her head. She said the first thing that came to mind. 'El Dorado, Senhora?'

The Senhora bit short her torrent of reproach. 'The El Dorado myth? That's an excellent idea, Inez, excellent.' Inez sighed with relief while Carlos rolled his eyes and stupid Alfredo mouthed '*Who?*' and Maro stared across at his sister in surprise. Still, their teacher was benign now, soothed and pacified.

Senhora Ferretti had once auditioned at the Manaus

Opera House, though she had not been accepted. She contented herself now giving recitals every third Sunday in the month in the church of Santa Barbara. 'It is nothing, whether one has an audience or not,' she would sometimes say. 'Music is life-enhancing. My life will always be richer for my singing.'

She held her little, dwindling class in thralls of terror: two dozen boys and girls who were all that remained of the Serra Vazia school. The parents of Serra Vazia delivered up their infants with awe and gratitude into the care of Senhora Ferretti. 'A fine woman. A cultured woman,' they said, but were glad it was their children and not they who had to spend each day in her classroom. The Ferretti voice rang out across the empty town, like a tocsin bell announcing the outbreak of battle: Senhora Ferretti's battle against Ignorance.

'Fools and drunkards!' said Mrs da Souza that night, hurling the tin plates on to the kitchen table. Maro had just put forward his explanation for why Enoque and Honorio Furtado might be digging a hole in the street outside. 'The world would be better off if they both put their fat heads in that hole and filled it in again!'

The light from the paraffin lamp in the centre of the table exaggerated all the creases in Mrs da Souza's face: made her look haggard, her face overlaid with prison bars of shadow. Her anger had begun with the failure of the mountain, but had grown so great that it no longer needed reasons to overspill. ('She is not angry with you,' their father used to whisper to Maro and Inez last thing at night. But it was sometimes hard to believe.) '*Garimpeiros!*' The family rounded their shoulders a little, pulling in their own heads like tortoises on the defensive. Like tortoises they munched on through the salad on their white enamel plates. Mrs da Souza had grown the salad, in tired earth, in an array of pots and planters which had the shop entirely surrounded: golden cooking oil tins, for the most part, painful to look at in the sun until they rusted. Picked in a rage, her salads contained increasingly strange ingredients: nettles and geraniums, gum wrappers blown off the street, clothes pegs fallen off the washing line.

The Baby, who could remember nothing different, sorted its salad enthusiastically into different shades of green. Always sorting, always sifting, it was. Inez thought it must be searching for a name, since Mrs da Souza would not give it one. Mrs da Souza considered it a waste to name a child before knowing whether it would survive. Her grandmother, she said, had named three children then buried them—three perfectly serviceable sets of names entombed in miniature coffins on the edge of the forest.

'Couldn't Great-Grandma have used the names again, once the children were dead?' asked Inez, being practical.

'And how would brother and sister be told apart in Heaven, may I ask? And the bad luck! Consider the bad luck!'

So the Baby continued to want for a name, in times so bad that it might wait for ever. Meanwhile it made little hoards—of bedfluff, pen tops, ring-pulls, always sorting, always collecting.

'Saving up for a name, maybe,' said Mr da Souza grinning. 'Like people collect cigarette tokens. Or Green Stamps.' But he did not say it within earshot of his wife.

The talk of gold—even though no one more sensible than Enoque and Honorio had started it—brought it all back to him: the memory of better times. 'In the days of the Rush there were a hundred-thousand here—up on the mountain. Spending money in the store. My father had two trucks a week coming in from Marabá.' Maro and Inez had heard it all countless times before, but would never have said so: the temporary enchantment lifted their father's face.

'It turned the mountain into a hell hole,' protested the lodger from behind his newspaper.

'Yes? So?' Mr da Souza broke out. 'In those days we had everything. Everything a man could want. Even things to complain about. Before the mountain failed.'

To say that the mountain failed suggests a sudden collapse, an implosion, a falling flat. That was not true, of course. The mountain still stood there, a backdrop to the town, scoured entirely bare of top soil, of trees, of scrub and bird life, its sides terraced by the open-cast mining. Once, briefly, Vazia Mountain in the Para region of Brazil, close by a tributary of the Xingu River, had been famous. It had made a few men into millionaires overnight, yielding huge nuggets of gold ore. Then it had made a great many men just rich enough to eat while they dug and sweated and dreamed of finding more.

Finally it had made men desperate, resentful, grubbing away at the mountain for enough gold-dust to survive. Some *garimpeiros* were still up there, scouring away at the empty mountain. But day after day the mountain failed them. That was what people meant when they talked about the mountain failing.

'Once we had scales in the shop—scales like a chemist. And Father would sell kilos of rice and flour for a peck of gold-dust,' said Mr da Souza dreamily. It had all happened a very long time ago. He did not really remember very much at all. Most of his memories had been told him afterwards by his parents. But he did remember being happy amid the filth, the mud, the dust, the greed. His father had been happy, and therefore the little boy at his feet had been happy. 'We were *needed* then,' he said proudly.

'You had *money* then,' said Mrs da Souza sourly, holding up a bus-ticket on the prongs of her fork, examining it with puzzled grief. 'Stop day-dreaming, da Souza. Your dreams come down on me like a slide of mud.'

7

And Mr da Souza apologized and reached out a hand and patted his wife's shoulder, so tenderly that the children looked away, pretending not to see. Anger at the dinner table is bad enough. Real sadness tastes much worse than bus-tickets or nettles.

Next day, Mrs da Souza went out at dawn to cook her bread dough at the bakery. In the no-light before dawn, while the air was as threadbare and dark as an army blanket, Maro and Inez, in their hammock beds, listened from overhead to the routine sounds of morning. They could hear The Baby spilling rice on to the floorboards to see where it would drop through. They could hear their mother telling The Baby not to do it. They could smell the dank yeast of the uncooked dough, which would come back after sunrise smelling of warmth. The noises were associated in their minds with that last sweet half-hour's idleness before the baked bread came back, wielded like a weapon by their always-angry mother.

They heard the inner door of the shop rattle, then the outer, insect door bang. They heard the same familiar, rotten planks in the boardwalk creak . . . then their mother cry out. Maro and Inez leapt out of bed and ran to the window.

Enoque and Honorio's hole had mysteriously grown since the night before, and now stretched clear across the entrance to the store. Although a plank had been thoughtfully laid across it, Mrs da Souza's feet had not found it in the darkness. She sat in the bottom of the hole, the dough settling into the contours of her lap.

As she stared up at them, a pair of headlamps lit her face, her mouth a perfect O of outrage and surprise. Enoque's old Jeep, its engine replaced, sped down the street, backfiring all the way. Its bald tyres crushed a Coke can then spurted it into the ditch, like a grenade into a shell-hole. Mrs da Souza put her hands over her head and called on the saints, as other people call on the fire brigade.

2

TRUTH AND CONSEQUENCES

What a thing that would be, eh? To find gold in a hole right outside your own front door. Go out. Pick up a handful of gold-dust and walk down to the juice bar. *Sucos* for all my friends! The idea deserved thinking about, however ludicrous it was. Maro and Inez found they could not put it out of their minds until someone told them categorically that it was nonsense.

So they asked Valmir the lodger, because he was an educated boy and was bound to know. Their mother was forever telling them how educated Valmir Zoderer was.

'No,' he said. 'I shouldn't think so for a minute. I don't know precisely what the geological indications would be if they were evident, but I think it far more likely to be the result of wishful thinking compounded by alcoholic delusion. And a good job too. We can do without *that* particular ecological disaster, thank you very much. Now I must get on. I'm writing to the President of the United Nations, you know.'

'Oh,' said Maro and Inez, and wished they had not asked. It had been good, just for a minute, to think of a hole outside the front door, with gold in it.

Valmir Zoderer lodged with the da Souzas, in a bedroom above the storeroom, and the children appreciated him because he helped with homework, though he was rather too serious to be fun. He had been expelled from Manaus University in his first term for writing a political letter to the student newspaper. He said that he had fled upriver to escape arrest and Mr and Mrs da Souza did not contradict him to his face. But behind his back, Mrs da Souza thought he was simply afraid to go home and see the disappointment in his parents' faces. All the same, she took him in. She ironed his shirts (which she never did for Mr da Souza) and as she rubbed salt into the ink stains on his cuffs she would tell Maro and Inez, 'You should spend time with Valmir. He's an educated boy. He knows things. You should listen to him.'

'Yesterday at dinner you said we mustn't,' said Maro, confused.

'Ah well, then he was talking *politics*.' The political opinions which came out of Valmir's mouth at mealtimes were deeply shocking to her Catholic soul, and she prayed for God to turn a deaf ear to them, too.

'And this morning you were saying how he mixes too much with *hobos*,' said Inez.

'Ah well. That's just his *letter-writing*.'

Valmir wrote letters all day long. He wrote them for other people, who had not the benefit of his education. And he wrote them for himself, to ease the ache in his heart, his regret that the world was not a better place. He never received replies, nor did his clients. But then whoever paid attention to a letter-writer? Mrs da Souza did not like the continual stream of illiterate farmers, miners, Indians, and squatters trooping up the outside stairs to Valmir's room, all wanting their letters written. But she paid for the stamps, even so, and as she stuck them on Valmir's mail, she would say to Maro and Inez, 'If only *your* handwriting were as beautiful as Valmir's. Valmir is writing to the United Nations. Fancy! You children should spend time with Valmir.'

Every evening they did so, which pleased their mother. But that was not why they did it.

When Valmir went up to watch the public television displayed in the square, the children went with him. He went to watch the News. They went to watch *Loony Toons*. He went there to pass loud, rude remarks criticizing the smiling politicians, doubting their honesty, heckling the TV set. Maro and Inez never stayed for the News, but left him shouting at the television and went and stood, with the other children, around the entrance to Disco Tony, listening to one of the twelve records on its juke box.

Despite a notice painted in car enamel on a brown-spotted mirror—'*A Slice of Rio!*'—Disco Tony was not glamorous. Even the children knew that. A string of Christmas lights hung across the door, but they had not lit up for years; the girls had stolen some of the bulbs for ear-rings, and the rest had blown. Empty cardboard cartons circled the building in a rising brown flood glistening with polythene surf. Just inside the door, behind a tubular table ringed with sticky marks, slept Tony, holding a reel of entrance tickets. The same reel had lasted him two years.

The children stood outside and listened. The records all dated from before they were born: Nat King Cole, Frank Sinatra, Doris Day, Howard Keel. But it did not matter. Time stood still at Tony's. Even the few customers moved only a very little to the music, jigging gently about in the stifling heat, gazing up at a black-painted ceiling daubed with moons and stars. Candlelight from the tables lit the eyes of the cockroaches gliding suavely by to the music of *Oklahoma*.

The noise mingled with that of the television, and the radios in the other juice bars on the square. There were no bars selling alcohol: it was forbidden because of the state mines close by: in the interests of public order, said the local police, drinking from hip flasks as they manned the roadblock just outside the town.

So it was a highly original sight to see Enoque and Honorio dancing in the square, both apparently as drunk as skunks. Arm in arm, shoulder to shoulder, they sidled, knees bent, in and out of the parked bicycles. They stamped and they whooped, they shouted out greetings to their neighbours as though they had just returned from years abroad. They grinned and guffawed. Enoque had something wrong with his hands so that when his hat fell

11

to the ground he made snatches at it—bowled it further along the ground—but could not get hold of its tatty brim. Maro, watching, felt compelled to pick up the wayward hat, at which Enoque rapped the top of his own bald, blotched head and cried, 'Cram it on there, son! Cram it on there! What a gentleman!'

As he did so, Maro sniffed eagerly. He had heard you could smell alcohol on a man's breath. But unfortunately, though Enoque smelt of many things, Maro had no way of knowing whether any of the smells were drink. How would he?

As he sniffed and coughed, Maro was caught round the neck by the effusive Enoque. 'You're a good friend, d'Souzzz. Good friend. Always were a good kid. When I'm rich, you can ride in my station wagon—nah!—camper-van. Like that, would you?' A brown ferret-like animal poked its head out through the hole where his shirt button was missing—a tayra with teeth like pins—and Maro pulled away in alarm. The animal also pulled in its head, and reappeared through another gap lower down. All Enoque's buttons were undone—everywhere—as though he had burst out of his clothes with sudden joy.

'Have you won the National Lottery, Senhor Furtado?'

Enoque thought for a while. 'Nah! But something just as good!' The black bristles of his unshaven face rubbed against Maro's face and left scratches.

Then his brother yanked him cheerfully away. 'Keep quiet, can't you! Didn't we agree? Keep it in as long as possible, eh? Keep our cards close to our chests.'

There was not a chance in the world of them keeping their happiness hidden. It spilled out like the straw out of scarecrows.

'Drunk! How disgusting,' said Inez priggishly, watching them reel down Main Street. 'Wait till Father Ignatius sees them.'

But they were not drunk. Or if they were, the Furtado brothers were drunk on Coca Cola and joy, a lethal

12

mixture fit to rob a man of all self-control, all respectable, Christian gloom. They plunged back into the hole outside Vazia Drugstore, holding their noses as if they were leaping into a blue lagoon. And so they were, in their imaginations.

Their laughter, coming from out-of-sight, below ground, had even more fascination than Tony's Disco, the TV, or Orlando's Juice Bar, and evening strollers from the square meandered down Main Street, irresistibly drawn. 'There is something *about* a hole,' said Tony aloud to himself, for even he had broken his permanent siesta to amble down the road. 'A world of possibilities in a hole.'

They stood, they looked, they chewed, and yet no one in the crowd called down to Enoque and Honorio. The two *garimpeiros* sat at either end of their excavation, like twin babies in a pram, trying to lob coffee beans into each other's mouth and giggling too much to manage it. It was Inez who asked the unspoken question on everyone's lips. Her high, imperious voice beside him made Maro jump. 'Have you found gold, then?' she called out.

Enoque pawed at his chest, his shaking fingertips incapable of picking up the beans accumulating there. He smiled the smile of a secretive sage, and tapped one finger to his nose. He missed, and that side-tracked him into trying to find the tip of his nose with little sideways swipes of his fingers, and a worried frown settled between his eyes. It was left for Honorio to say, with all the enigmatic mystery of Bugs Bunny, 'Might've, mightn't we?'

A sharp thrill shook both Maro and Inez unlike any they had ever felt before. A murmur ran through the little crowd of onlookers. They eyed each other. Some instinctively looked at their watches, as if time, from now on, would be of the essence. Inez turned to ask Valmir what he had to say now, but found the lodger was missing. Looking back up towards the square, she saw him completely engrossed in the six o'clock news, oblivious of being all alone, and with his back turned on the real news of the day.

The juke box in Tony's disco made its own quaint contribution:

> 'There's a brigh~~t~~ golden haze on the meadow!
> There's a bright golden haze on the ...'

In the next few days, Mr da Souza had unusually large numbers of customers at the Vazia Drugstore. Strangers from out of town. None wanted to buy much, but all felt obliged to make some small purchase, then hesitated to leave. 'It's just a joke, isn't it?' they would say, cocking their heads towards the shop doorway. 'All this digging. Just somebody's idea of a joke.'

Inez and Maro, sitting over their homework in the stockroom, lifted their heads and listened intently for their father's reply. Mr da Souza said:

'Second biggest gold reef in the world. That's what the geologists said back during the Last Rush. Second biggest gold reef. Funny if none of it stretched this way, eh? The odd seam. The odd few thousand tons?'

In the storeroom, the children stared at one another. When the shop doors closed they dashed into the shop. 'Is it true, then, Dad? There is gold!'

'Ah, well . . . now . . . my little chickens . . . ' Mr da Souza was embarrassed. He had not known they were listening. He did not like to be caught lying by his own children; it did not seem a good example to set. 'You don't want to go believing everything . . . '

'Then why did you say it?' asked Inez.

'We-e-ell . . . What else am I going to say? Nonsense, of course, but how would it help trade to say it. Talk like that . . . Even the *rumour* of gold . . . it'd bring the crowds flocking. They'll come from Marabá—nosey folk, curious folk, maybe a geologist or two, even. Just trippers, maybe. Denying it . . . well, how would that help the shop any, eh? D'you see?'

An Indian child came in for manioc flour, offering up a

14

twig basket in exchange. Just for once, the child spoke. 'Papa says is it true *alicanto* bird seen in trees? Shining? And *carbunco*?'

Out in the storeroom, Inez and Maro sniggered into their pencil boxes. The mythical *alicanto* birds supposedly ate gold and glowed with the brightness of it when their stomachs were full. The *carbunco* was supposedly a tortoise-like animal with a double shell which it could open and shut (like a larder door) to take on fresh supplies of its favourite food: gold. To think that there were people out there who *believed* in such beasts!

To their utter astonishment they heard their father reply, 'For sure. Saw two myself. Bright as headlamps. Two *carbuncos* drinking down at the river.' Maro jumped to his feet, but Inez restrained him with a hand on his arm. She was shocked to hear her father telling lies, but she understood why now. How would it help trade to deny the rumours of *alicantos* and *carbuncos*? Confirm them, and more Indians would arrive in Vazia in the hope of finding gold. Some might even have a little money to spend in the shop.

And what if it *were* to start up all over again, that fever of his half-remembered youth? The Gold Rush. Other grown-ups remember their childhood as golden with sunshine. Mr da Souza remembered his as sunny with gold. The shop could only benefit, surely, from 'Enoque's Find', whether the rumours lasted a week or a year, and even though they were false. He was going to climb aboard the wave of speculation, like a surfer mounting a wave, and ride it for all it was worth.

So his children heard him say to people in the shop, 'Second biggest reef of gold in the world, that's all I know. Must be something left down there. Stands to reason, doesn't it?' And the customers would suddenly remember urgent business and rush out, leaving the shop door and its fly screen clapping like a pair of hands behind them. Clap clap clap.

Mr da Souza could have applauded, too. He could have cheerfully raised three cheers for the Furtado brothers and what they had done for Vazia town. He could even forgive them the fact that the street outside his door now had so many bunkers in it, it was no longer passable to traffic.

3

FOFOCA

(The time of rumour)

How did the word get about? Apart from Mr da Souza's enthusiastic exaggeration, how did the word spread?

Peasant Radio, they call it, but there are no radios involved. It is simply a matter of one man mentioning it out loud and being overheard by another on his way to the city. And then the second calls in at a city bar or barber's or bank and chances to mention it. And a woman hearing him, whose sister's husband is a member of the Brazilian Gold Diggers Association takes home the news. And so the sister's husband mentions it at a union meeting. And the *donos* hear of it—the men with a little money saved up and a hunger to make more. A miner comes to his *dono* saying he cannot make the latest repayment on his gear. 'Have you tried Serra Vazia?' the answer goes. 'They say there's a seam of gold left from the main reef—overlooked—under the main street of the town.'

And, of course, there are certain words in the language that have the power to burn themselves into a man's imagination. They fire him with the irresistible desire to leave his family, take his Jeep and his friends or sons or neighbours down a thousand miles of dirt track, and sweat and break his back in a hole in the road. One of those words is *Gold*.

It is called *fofoca*, that time of rumour and raised hopes, of exaggeration and lies, of racing against time to find a piece of ground where no one else's pick has fallen yet.

They say the word of God spread like that once. Unstoppable. Its ideas left the early Christians gasping at

17

the unimaginably wonderful possibilities of forgiveness, everlasting life, and a place in Heaven among the angels. A nightless eternity of golden sunlight.

Unfortunately, by the time Father Ignatius got up into the pulpit of Santa Barbara Church in Serra Vazia, nothing he could find to say had enough magic in it. Standing in the pulpit, looking down at his congregation, he did not believe that a single soul was even listening to him.

'"Beware!" said Our Lord. "Guard against greed: a man's life is more than the sum of his possessions!"' He scooped the words out over the pulpit rail as though he were bailing out a sinking boat. He told them the parable of the rich farmer who planned a wealthy retirement only to be told he must die the same night. He pleaded with the people in front of him to store up treasures in Heaven: '"For where your treasure is, there is your heart also!"'. . . Don't you see what'll happen otherwise?'

The young priest had a shiningly soft and golden wealth of hair. It curled about his temples and moved, like a field of windy wheat, as he darted his head this way and that. Blonds were an unusual sight on the Amazon. Though the physical characteristics of Brazilians vary more than anywhere in the world, still a blond, a true blond, is a rare sight, and his appearance had always helped Father Ignatius along. It gave him a charisma, especially with the women, who thought him a *lovely* boy—quite lovely—chattering away up there: an angelic figure suspended, in a carved wooden chariot, flying half-way between floor and roof of the church. He was quite wrong to suppose no one was interested. Inez da Souza, for instance, cared about very little else in the whole world.

The church of Santa Barbara was built of brick, unlike most of the wooden town, but had a corrugated tin roof. Now and then a rattle of water, like heavy rain, fell on the tin or rapped at the windows as if a gale were in progress outside, and Father Ignatius would flinch visibly. 'Does not

Saint Matthew tell us how wealth chokes the Word of God as weeds and thorns choke the growing corn? Does he not warn us: "You can't serve two masters"?'

This was patently true, for those who had come to Mass that morning could not be out digging. And those who had not, were out there now, this minute, exploiting every second. There was a great herd of men standing at the rear of the church, filling the nave with the smell of sweat, who were longing to be gone. They felt a superstitious need to attend church: God would bless them for it. But Lord! how the priest did blather on, keeping them from their *barrancos*. What was he drivelling about anyway? Wasn't Santa Barbara the patron saint of miners? Would *she* have stood in the pulpit telling them they ought not to dig? If only he would get on to the Blessing and shut up.

Inez da Souza heard nothing of their shifting and trampling and grumbling. She saw nothing of The Baby collecting up all the Sunday-best shoes women had slipped off beneath their chairs. She saw only Father Ignatius, was spellbound by the beauty of his wrath, by the sunny halo around his anger. Usually he was pleasant, smiling, and confident. She had never seen him like this, agitated to the point of sorrow, beautiful in his grief, as some crucifixes are beautiful. In fact, watching Father Ignatius, arms out to either side, hands trembling, eyes thrown up to Heaven, there was hardly any distinguishing, for Inez, between her priest and her Saviour.

'Consider, children, how hard it is for the rich to enter the Kingdom of God . . . easier for a camel to go through the eye of a needle!'

Oh yes, she believed him! Outside the church's closed doors was living proof. Every day another Jeep skidded to a halt at the barriers across Main Street and emptied out another handful of miners who struggled to squeeze their equipment through the obstacle course of *moinhos* and chutes. *She* would not turn heathen. *She* would never worship the Golden Calf. She would live by every word

19

which proceeded out of the mouth of Father Ignatius. She pulled the lace veil a little higher over her hair and thanked God for sending her town such a saintly man, such a fine man, such a golden shining example. She forgot that she had ever been excited by the thought of gold in a hole outside her door. For Father Ignatius said that gold was an Evil Thing.

' . . . *For is not the love of money the root of all evil? . . .* '

Beside her, her parents sat glowing with righteous happiness. Like Noah and his family, the da Souzas floated in their church pew, safe from the Chaos all around, blessed by God beyond all their wildest hopes. Even if they did not quite understand what was wrong with digging for gold, they were above criticism anyway. For Mr da Souza had not so much as picked up a spade. He had simply stood behind his shop counter and served an ever-growing queue of customers. He had sold salt fish and canned peaches, nails and hammers, K13 to repel mosquitos, and Colestase to cure diarrhoea. He had sold them cups and boots, medallions of Saint Barbara, and cards to gamble with. He had sold them cigarettes and mosquito nets, underpants, and maps of Vazia which he sat up nightly to copy off an old Transbraziliano bus map. Mr da Souza was a profoundly happy man, prospering from other men's eagerness to dig up his street.

His wife, too, could look up at the young man in the pulpit and take delight in his wheaten hair, curling beard, and blazing rhetoric. Her husband's business was thriving and she saw no need to defy the priest's advice not to give way to the gold fever, not to dig.

'*For is not the love of money the root of all evil?*' demanded Father Ignatius with agonized desperation. Inez nodded eagerly, and Father Ignatius saw her and smiled sadly down at her so that her heart turned over inside her.

In front of the Holy Virgin's statue, instead of just one or two of the electric candles being lit in supplication, every last bulb flickered its orange filament. Each represented the prayers of *garimpeiros* for success in their prospecting. Maria Monica Manoel, wishing to light a candle for the recovery of her sick son, had had to leave her ten centavos lying on the table top: there was no candle slot left free. Ignatius, catching sight of that small, patient coin, seemed unable to look away from it, and his homily petered out. With a final gasp of exasperation, he barked out a hymn number at the congregation, and the portable organ wheezed and staggered into a hymn:

'*Dear Lord and Father set us free . . .* '

This one morning, Father Ignatius wanted no one's freedom as much as his own. Why had God sent him here, to watch the things that were about to happen? Why had God given him the wits to foresee what was going to happen, and then left him powerless to prevent it?

The da Souza family stirred with pride as little Maro, in a white surplice, brought the gift plate of holy wafers and handed them to the priest. The light from the blaze of electric candles reflected off the plate and lit up Maro's face as though with angelic light, and the magic of the Mass rolled on, too slowly for some, too fast for others.

When, at the end, the doors opened on to the street, the scene outside was revealed afresh, with a new vividness, to those who had gone into church only an hour before. Santa Barbara Church stood at the opposite end of Main Street from the square and had once enjoyed a seedy vista all the way down to the public TV set.

But the square was not visible now. A sort of street market of wooden structures had pitched itself in the way: chutes and gantries aswarm with men. Hosepipes squirmed and coiled in among them like giant worms disturbed by digging.

Digging.

For there was gold. Not very much, as yet. A few ounces, no more. But the very presence of gold—however little—meant the next spadeful might contain an ingot big as a frog, might change a man overnight into a millionaire.

So the street's yellow crust of soil, compacted over the years by countless feet, had been smashed with picks, then prised up in clods. High-pressure hoses, mounted on the gantries and pointed down into the ground, cut open the street with lances of silver water. The loosened earth was being shovelled into wheelbarrows or sacks or directly into mechanical crushers—the *moinhos*—whose racket obliterated every other noise with shuddering screams of rollers crushing stones. A giant chewing on the bones of his victims could not have achieved such noises. And as the solid rock resisted the rollers, the whole oil-drum encasing the machinery shook and juddered as if the earth inside were dying violently. Now and then the hoses would be pointed at the sky while the diggers loosened and shovelled and bagged their workings; and the sunlit geysers would cloak the street in rainbows, and the spray would rattle on the church's tin roof, its painted glass windows, the wooden facias of the shops and houses.

A trench two metres deep already wound its way between the boardwalks, one hole melting into another. The original pot-holes made by Enoque and Honorio had been lost without trace, had been eaten up by the greater hole.

The gangs worked in fives—two wrestling with the hose to direct its high-pressure jet into the gravel subsoil. Gasping amid the scattering spray and bouncing gravel, two men with garden forks dug out the big stones and heaved them aside. The fifth had charge of the *chupadeira*, a great, slurping, ravenous nozzle that sucked up the loosened gravel with a never-ending greed and spewed it out at the other end into a ladder of mesh-bottomed boxes resting on pieces of carpet.

Inez recognized one piece of carpet—blue with silver flowerheads. Mr Gomez had ordered it through the drugstore and her father had trucked it in from Marabá for him. Mr Gomez had carried it home over his shoulder—blue and silver flowerheads—a present for his wife on their twenty-fifth wedding anniversary. Now it was back in the street—at least a section of it—sold through the window, presumably, for a few centavos. Beneath the *caixas*, its colours quickly changed to brown, but its pile stood erect awaiting, awaiting the very slight chance of a spangling of gold.

So what if the floors of Serra Vazia town lay bare and carpetless? There was no time for dancing just now, in any case. There was hardly even time to draw breath, to come to terms with the stampede of newcomers.

As brown as cows they were, irrespective of the colour of their skin. There were *mulatos* and *cariocas* and *gauchos* and *caboclos* but their clothes had all gathered the same covering of dust and mud. And they had the desperation of mad bullocks, too, plunging into their trench, plunging out of it again, wild-eyed, whenever a piece of equipment broke, the diesel ran dry, or a rock choked the *chupadeira*.

Startled by the sudden arrival of all these strangers, the people living on Main Street first huddled together in neighbourly knots, telling each other that some of the gold must belong to them by rights. 'A man with a river bank, now he owns the river bed as far out as half-way—I'm sure that's the law. I'm sure he does. Pretty sure, anyway. Does he? Isn't it the same with a street? Is it?'

But although they were in total agreement that Serra Vazia's gold ought to belong to Serra Vazia, still there was no stopping the frenzied grubbing about of strangers beyond their boardwalks. The only way of assuring that the gold came into local hands was to get out there and dig. That was why Inez could recognize her neighbours as well as her neighbours' carpets sweltering and labouring in the earthworks, wearing the brown mud disguise of the *garimpeiro*. She shook her head at the sight of them, sighing and sorry that they should fly in the face of Father Ignatius's holy advice.

Mrs da Souza shook more than her head. She shook a broom at them. Not that she wanted the miners to go:

Heaven forbid they should stop spending their money in the store and in the town. God forbid that these Times of Plenty should come to an end. But she did sit on her boardwalk all day to make sure no one was careless enough to damage her flower blooms or squander mud on her clean planks. And she did *wish* gold could be brought to the surface by some *cleaner* process. She envisaged fondly somehow, a great bulldozer proceeding, at stately speed, down Main Street filling in the pot-holes, ending the excitement but making straight the way (like in the Psalms) restoring peace and cleanliness, sweeping all the dirt and the machinery and the *garimpeiros* into a single pile of rubbish on the football pitch.

Not to complain. Everything in her shop was selling. Even a consignment of spare hub-caps was selling now: not to car-owners but for use as *cuias* and *bateias*—bowls for gold-panning. The bowls were for use down at the river.

There, too, the landscape was greatly changed. For *fofoca* had whispered in a thousand destitute ears: if there was gold under the town, might there not be gold in the town's river? Boatloads of the poorest Indians and *peãos* had arrived and camped along the banks, stringing their hammocks between the trees. It put a stop to fishing for Inez and Maro, who had liked to go there on quiet afternoons after school and catch piranha with little pieces of Fray Bentos. Already the river had been churned into a muddy wallow, where whole families grubbed about, shovelling, riddling, and panning the silt. Their faces were blank, spoke neither hope nor excitement. When nothing surrendered itself out of the endless wormy mud they showed no disappointment, no fury at having been brought, on false pretences, to this cattle drink in the middle of nowhere. It had all happened to them before.

Next time he visited the river, Maro brought a *cuia* from the store. He had no idea what to do with it, but it was fun just mudlarking in the water, swirling the gravel and earth round and round in the dish till it slopped out over his trousers and bare feet.

'Stop that at once!' said his sister, knocking the bowl out of his hands. 'You heard Father Ignatius. It's wrong to dig.'

'I wasn't digging. I was panning,' said Maro sulkily. 'And what's wrong with it anyway? What's he got against gold? Just 'cos he doesn't need money doesn't mean to say everybody else couldn't do with some.'

'It's the root of all evil,' said Inez in a righteous tone. 'Father Ignatius says it will make people . . . Well, he says people won't go to Heaven who . . . It ought to be enough just that he says it!' concluded Inez hotly. The less sure she was of herself, the more haughty she became. To tell the truth, she did not fully understand why Father Ignatius was so against the digging. She had not dozed off while he explained—no, no, not once! She could remember exactly how he had *looked* every second of the time, when the blond curls broke across his ear, where his hair parted, how his lashes were darker and where the creases of his nose ended. It upset her that she could not remember his argument quite so clearly—even if only to answer Maro's silly questions. But she could only push her brother roughly and confiscate his panning dish, telling him, 'If Father Ignatius says it's wrong, then it's wrong.'

Maro ground his teeth. He was frankly sick of the sound of Father Ignatius. The name kept finding its way into Inez's conversation. It popped up from behind her litter-strewn lettuce, jumped out from her hammock just as he was dozing off; it was even scrawled in ink on the cover of his sister's notebooks. It had been the same when she became best friends with Mundicarmo. 'Mundicarmo says this.' 'Mundicarmo likes that.' 'Mundicarmo never goes out in the rain without overshoes.' 'Mundicarmo has a red coral bracelet and a brother in the Azores.' Maro could see it annoyed the lodger too, this obsession with the priest. Valmir was a socialist. Valmir was a humanist. Valmir did not go to church on Sundays! Valmir said religion was a plot and that all priests were liars. Perhaps Valmir would be his ally, against Inez and her tedious, 'Father Ignatius wouldn't like it.' 'Father Ignatius says we mustn't.'

Then Valmir proved to be just as mad as both of them. Take the birthday party.

For Mr da Souza's birthday, they all went to the *churrascaria* in the square, where huge spits of meat were brought to the table in an endless procession. The waiter crowned Mr da Souza with a Mexican sombrero and sang him the Birthday Salute while he grinned sheepishly out from under the brim.

The tables both inside and outside the once-deserted grill-bar were crowded with *garimpeiros* who had been breaking their backs turning and sifting earth all day. On the edge of the square, men squatted about like beggars with begging bowls. But on closer inspection they all held butane torches, and now and then, with a sudden venomous hiss and a burst of flame so bright it left its mark on the eyeball, they directed their torches on to the contents of metal panning dishes. Peculiar fumes drifted over and mixed with the smell of roasting meat.

'Well,' said Mr da Souza, from under the hat. 'I never thought last year that there'd be much to celebrate in this birthday of mine . . . ' His wife reached out and touched his arm tenderly. The lines were gone from her face as if the heat from the restaurant's grill had melted them all away. 'If things carry on this way in the store . . . '

Suddenly Valmir got to his feet. The family thought he was going to make a speech. Inez noticed how nervous he must be, for when he took hold of the table top, the whole table shook. Mrs da Souza looked pleased and grateful, beaming her approval at Valmir. But he was looking directly over her head, and when he opened his mouth it was to shout across the square at the squatting men with the butane torches. 'Don't you know anything? Don't you care that people are eating here? Those fumes—don't you know what they can do to you?' He jibbered with helpless

26

fury, the table dancing on its four legs, clinking the glasses, slopping the juice. 'Poison your own wives! Poison your own children! But keep your damned smoke out of our noses! What's the matter with you? Do you people never learn from the past? What's the matter with you? Go away! Leave us alone! Who asked you to come here?'

There was a very brief lull in the noise, though the television continued to drone out a soap drama in American with subtitles, and down in Disco Tony, Frank Sinatra was singing 'My Way'.

Easy-going Mr da Souza tipped his birthday sombrero further forward over his face for a hiding place. Mrs da Souza called for the bill, pressing cooling fingers against her shamed cheeks and glaring at Valmir.

Here and there around the square, a woman with a baby on her knee pulled her shawl across its face to keep out the smoke fumes. But the menfolk did not see. They were too busy wagging scornful hands, yelling at Valmir to sit down and shut up. The local men snarled and sneered and laughed loud and long. So the letter-writer agreed with the priest, did he? And they had always thought the two hated each other: priest and socialist.

Money, the root of all evil? They could hardly credit that anyone believed in that old lie any more. Every sane 'grown-up' in Serra Vazia knew full well the cause of the world's evils. All the evils in their own lives stemmed from being poor: from grinding, inescapable, everyday, everlasting poverty. These visiting miners were already bringing prosperity back to the town. Scraps of money. Wisps of hope. If they found large deposits of gold, that prosperity would turn to wealth. And who but a madman turns up his nose at wealth? After all, people say the floors of Heaven are tiled with beaten gold. So God must like the stuff.

4

VANITY FAIR

'Don't he want to get rich?' said Enoque to Maro.

'I don't think he likes a mess,' said Maro vaguely. Although he had been obliged to listen to Valmir Zoderer's arguments every night at dinner, he had made no more sense of them than that: Valmir did not like a mess. He did not want all those trees keeling over into the river because their roots had been blasted loose by jets of water. He did not want all that mud in the town street. He did not want the miners making a disagreeable smell with their butane torches and their latrines. 'If you ask me, he's a snob,' said Maro. 'He likes peace and quiet for reading his books. It's too noisy for him now.'

'All the same. You'd think he'd want to get rich.' Enoque was an easy-going soul, slow to condemn anyone out-of-hand. His huge experience of the world had rendered him more generously tolerant of people's differences than Maro. He was simply bewildered by the student's (and the priest's) determination to be miserable and angry. There was the rest of the town, revelling in its new-found wealth, putting on all the splendour of a *carnaval* float; and there were Valmir and Ignatius, both carping, both haranguing hapless passers-by like Cassandra running about the streets of Troy insisting it will one day be destroyed. (No one believed her, either.) 'It's not even as if they agree with each other!' Enoque wailed. It did distress him that they could not be happy. He was deafened by such a symphony of happiness himself that he wanted the whole world to sing and dance to the music. Enoque and his brother were considered the *desbravadors* of the gold strike: the pioneer heroes who had opened up the earth's crust in just the right place for everyone to plunge in their hands and grasp riches.

In actual fact, the seam under Vazia town was not proving to be quite the glittering reef *fofoca* had suggested. In actual fact there proved so far to be just ten ounces of gold per ton of soil. But to complain at that seemed to Enoque like spitting in the eye of God who, in His infinite bounty, had made the Furtado Brothers heroes of Serra Vazia. There was even talk of Honorio standing as socialist candidate in the forthcoming local elections.

Men bought Enoque drinks now, read aloud newspaper articles for him (for there was something the matter with his eyes) and even fastened his fly buttons for him when his wretched fingers let him down. And now that people reverently asked his opinion, in the juice bars, he proved an extraordinarily interesting man—at least to Maro who would hover nearby and drink in Enoque's reminiscences. Maro sought him out in his every spare minute, offered to help on the *barranco* (that grand title given to the five-by-five-metre hole where Enoque and Honorio dug). Maro liked to see the loose gravel come rattling out of the *chupadeira* into the *caixas*, the stones and sand and gravel rolling over the mesh, the heavier gold falling through into the pile of the carpet underneath. He could watch it for hours: the water, the rolling gravel, the drenched tips of carpet with pattern of flowers still just visible. And the voices of Enoque and Honorio would be telling him about their days treasure hunting among the graves of the Incans or diamond mining on Mount Roraima, the Lost World of Senhor Arthur Conan Doyle. As the carpet was combed of its dandruff of dirty gold, Maro would give over his own imagination to thinking how he might spend each grain if it were his.

Enoque was good company—much better than pompous Valmir the Griper or Inez the little Puritan. 'I know why *she* does it,' Maro confided in Enoque, man-to-man. '*She's* against the digging because *he* says he doesn't like it. Father *Ignatius*. Whatever *he* says, *she* says.' He rocked his head from side to side, mimicking, and pulled a face. A gulf was deepening between brother and sister as wide and deep as the trench in Main Street.

Inez, meanwhile, sat at her desk in that position of trust at the back of the room of Serra Vazia School, biting her lip. Her face was turned down over an open book, but her eyes were watching, through her top lashes, Senhora Ferretti enthroned before an empty classroom. Even papery El Dorado shivered with alarm at the turn events had taken.

At first, the children had come to school as usual, picking their way between the *barrancos* or through the back streets, to foregather, as noisy as crows, along the school wall.

'Have you seen the new TV in the square?'

'Who cares? My dad says we'll get one of our own pretty soon.'

'Mine's going to get me a cassette player.'

'And guess whose music you'll be playing.'

'Well, she *is* the greatest! She just is.'

Their taste in music had been the first thing to change. Tony's had replaced its juke-box with a disco-complex that could pound out music at a hundred decibels. *Oklahoma* was incompatible. Marilyn Monroe was dead. Rock music crashed through Tony's now like a breaking wave, and appeared to shatter against the walls in visibly whirling silver fragments. For Tony had bought a mirror ball. It spun from the ceiling, reflecting the roving spotlights which were synchronized to the thump of the amplifiers. The new sign over the door read '*Movimentado*' ('where the action is'), pumping never-ending sections of light along transparent tubular letters. It hypnotized and mesmerized, that moving light flowing through those enormous letters. The children were drawn to it as minnows are to the jaws of the angler fish by the glowing lure dangling over the entrance.

A huge, menacing, newly employed bouncer, hunch-backed with muscles, swiped at them with gorilla grunts and long gorilla arms. But his swearing and fists could not scatter the children for long. They regrouped and drifted back. The music both filled their souls with a new excitement and emptied their heads of the power to think. Later they sat sipping *sucos* in the juice bars, their heads still bouncing in time to the remembered music.

Once upon a time, they had tasted the exquisite pleasure of *sucos* only on feast-days and birthdays. Now their parents, too busy digging up their yards or trading with miners to cook meals, packed their children off with money for 'treats' at Orlando's, where the boys and girls stood and watched the new liquidizer spin ice and sugar and whole passion fruits or limes into a drink fit for the gods.

They were almost gods, after all. They were heirs to a reef of gold. Their town was built right on top of it! Their futures towered up as glittering as Aeolia, the mytholo-gical kingdom with walls of brass. When they looked at their reflections in the new pink mirrors fixed to the walls of Orlando's, each saw El Dorado, King of the Juice Bars, and carried himself differently, strutting with kingly pride.

At first they thought of school as an unfortunate interference with the urgent business of digging, listening to music, and drinking *sucos*. They fidgeted and pined restlessly at the need to waste six hours a day in thrall to Senhora Ferretti. Then some of the parents, finding they needed extra hands on the *barrancos*, took their children out of school . . . 'Just for a day or two . . . ' Others were gone from the classroom next morning. The ones remaining chafed resentfully up and down their desk seats, looking out of the windows, listening to the incessant noise of the *moinhos* crushing rocks, and whispering wild rumours to one another about the size of the fortunes being made.

'A thousand dollars for ten grammes! D'you know what that looks like? Nothing! A half a bar of chocolate! A thousand bucks!'

'I know what I'd do with a thousand! I'd get myself a Suzuki with a windshield down here and handlebars way down there . . .'

Senhora Ferretti's voice chimed out with greater and greater strident urgency: the tocsin bell warning of disaster. But if her boy pupils did not quite lose their terror of her, they soon discovered the next best protection: to stay away, with or without their parents' permission, and to hang about the *barrancos* feeling like men.

La Senhora sent Letters Home deploring this interruption to school routine, questioning the wisdom of letting children mix with dubious strangers. She drew the parents' attention to the safety hazards outside the school walls, and hinted darkly at 'corrupting influences'.

'You must go to school,' said Mr da Souza sternly to Maro. 'Senhora Ferretti is a great lady—almost an opera singer! She deserves your respect.'

But when Maro came home and said he was the only boy left in the class, Mr da Souza could see how impossible the situation was for his son. A boy's 'machismo' could never survive such a fate: to be the only boy left among girls. And he allowed Maro to cut school, adding in a whisper, 'Just so long as your mother doesn't hear about it.'

Strange how different school looked from the other side of the railings. All of a sudden the boys could laugh out loud at La Senhora's absurd rules: *No shoes beyond the door. No packed lunches to be eaten without a plate.* No permission to leave while one paintbrush remained unwashed, one book spine protruded from the shelves, one desk lid rested proud of an untidy desk.

The street, the *real* world, was a kingdom of mud, the richest men the ones who could rip their way quickest into the bowels of the earth and never mind the mess. A man did not *tidy up* after a real day's work: he looked around with satisfaction at the heaps of soil worked and discarded like so many wormcasts. The real men were the ones who did not mind digging through a town's sewage—who could make a joke of it—and jokes much dirtier than that, too. The *garimpeiros* from out of town had seen a thing or two. They were about as different from Senhora Ferretti as creatures can be within the one species.

What was she, after all? Comical mountain of a woman, thinking to intimidate the world beneath with the great overhang of her bosom and the avalanche of her voice. Disappointed spinster scraping by on a pittance. As soon as they saw that—that one huge difference between themselves and Senhora Ferretti—that was when they fully grasped the worthlessness of her and her run-down school. For Senhora Ferretti had nothing—a salary so eaten up by the rising cost of living that she would never afford another new dress. She had an upstairs apartment on Main Street (so no garden to dig up for gold) and a figure so laughable that it would have taken block-and-tackle to lower her into a *barranco*. *They* were going to be rich: Alfredo and Carlos, Lucio, Paul and Raimundo. Maro.

School had nothing to do with success. And that above all made them jeer with contempt whenever they heard the Senhora's operatic tones wafting down from the school house. For she had tried to fool them, hadn't she? She had told them, 'Attend to your lessons, or you'll never get on in the world.' What a lie! What a con trick! She shouldn't look so surprised, should she, to have clods of mud thrown at her as she picked her way home from school at night, or to find her windows broken by stones? The woman was a fraud.

What it took for a man to get on in the world was a fork, a hose, a riddle, and a pump: to work till the mud crawled down between vest and skin: to get lucky and to keep his eyes set on that first thousand dollars.

33

Even the girls found out the truth after a week or two. School was a time-wasting irrelevance: one envious old bat's attempt to trick them out of enjoying themselves and getting rich. One by one the girls, too, disappeared from Serra Vazia School.

'We should perhaps continue with our preparations for Independence Day,' said Senhora Ferretti to a classroom containing only two girls. It was odd: in an empty room her voice should have boomed louder than ever. Instead it sounded muffled and a little tremulous.

'D'you think there'll still be an Independence Day, Senhora?' asked Mundicarmo timidly.

'Observe the calendar!' her teacher came back at her. 'Can you suggest a way in which we may pass from the sixth of September to the eighth without entertaining the existence of Independence Day? Man may uproot his habitat, overturn the laws of civilized behaviour, but he cannot, as yet, alter the ordered sequence of Time! If you mean, "Will there still be an Independence Day parade?" my opinion is that some things, for good or ill, are indispensible to the Brazilian way of life. And parades—holidays—excuses for excess are some of them . . . By the way, since we are such a very *select* gathering today, perhaps Senhorinha da Souza would care to move forward into one of these empty desks at the front. I see no need to strain my voice.'

'There's enough to celebrate, God knows!' said Mr da Souza sitting down to his Sunday dinner. The *feijoada* his wife placed before them was an expression of joy in itself. Pork sausage and smoked meat, black beans, and slices of orange bobbed together in the pot; the family's heads spun in the garlic fumes. Beneath the table, Maro scuffed the studs of his new football boots, savouring the fiery discomfort of his feet. He had exchanged his altar boy's white surplice for a white T-shirt and shorts. The football pitch awaited him, its grass freshly cut. The *garimpeiros* and their children were so plentiful in Vazia now that several football teams had formed spontaneously, and all afternoon they would play matches with each other until the daylight failed and the winners dropped with exhaustion.

Mr and Mrs da Souza were going dancing. A peasant band, roused by the rhythmic thump of the machinery, had declared the intention to play *forró* music in the square.

'They play *tropicalismo* down at Orlando's now,' said Maro gleefully, knowing it would spark a yearning in Valmir so keen that his heart would ache all afternoon.

'I can live without it,' said Valmir, poring over a sheet of paper, editing, altering. 'I lived without it before: I can live without it now.'

'But what *for*, dear?' said Mrs da Souza, pushing bowls of bread and stew and salad towards him so that his paperwork was edged off the table. 'I'm sure it's very *nice* music. And it would do you good to get out and dance. It does everyone good to dance. Or go to the football! Go and see Maro play.'

'I have something to finish.'

'More letters?'

'Just something.'

Mrs da Souza sighed. She was starting to lose patience with her lodger. After lunch, she sprinkled her hair with perfume, crayoned her mouth a fiery red, and went to dance in the square, her best shoes rap-tapping along the boardwalk. She held her husband on her arm like a knight's shield, fending off the offensive sight of upheaval and sweaty toil in the street.

The work Valmir really wanted to finish was a poem. He would never have admitted to writing poetry (although it is a manly enough thing to do) but because, even before he unclogged his ballpoint with angry little swirls and screwed his fingers into his hair, he could see that it would do no good.

There was a town where once upon a time
There lived the poor, the honest, and the free
Against the forest and the summer's shine
With flowing river watering the trees.
But there arose a dragon from the past,
With blazing eyes and scales of jagged steel,
Roaring its way out of the ruined, vast
Spaces ploughed up by its heels.
It came and spat its poison in the stream.
It came and fouled the forest with its dirt.
It burned and scalded landscapes with its steam,
And what it did not kill, it maimed and hurt.
It dug, as dogs dig, mindlessly, dug deep—
Nor rested from destruction night or day.
For its conscience was too horrible for sleep
Since it murdered everything within its way.

Still, the people worshipped the dragon
and prayed for it to stay.

Valmir took his poem, pierced an inky hole through a top
corner and found a piece of string in the storeroom. Then
he opened the back door on to Lisboa Avenue, meaning to
see as little as possible of the digging on his way to the
square.

Unfortunately, two new *barrancos* had just been dug in
Lisboa Avenue. Two crews of *garimpeiros* were opening up
a new frontier of the Serra Vazia Goldfield. They had taken
two of Mrs da Souza's gold oil-cans to prop up their
caixas, half emptying them to make them easier to carry.
The discarded flowers lay in the roadway, their heads just
sticking out from under the mound of earth dug out from
the holes. When Valmir remonstrated with the *garimps*,
they swore at him vilely. When he turned away, they threw
a clod of earth at him which broke against the back of his
head.

When he reached the square, the *forró* was well
underway. He saw Mrs da Souza, dancing with the happy

abandon of a woman without worries, and he realized that his landlady was much younger than he had ever guessed. The peasant music stirred him. Perhaps, after all, he would join in, and dance with Mrs da Souza to prove that he was not an entirely joyless individual.

Then, to his astonishment, he found that his was not the only poem strung from the bracket holding the new, giant, colour TV.

This was the traditional place for the town's poets to hang their 'string literature'. The Buddhists pin their prayers to wheels so that the wind may carry their prayers to heaven. The Brazilians tie up their feelings by string to dance in the breeze: love poems, patriotic poems, poems of protest . . . But as far as he knew, Valmir was the only poet *in* Vazia. So he was amazed to find a sheet of white paper already fluttering where he had intended to hang his. No one but Valmir had ever hung his poems beneath the TV set before. There were so few people in Vazia who could or would read them. He ran a curious eye over the other poem.

> *The gods of Greece took gold from the sun's heart,*
> *Plunging their fists deep into the knot of fire*
> *To grasp the seeds whose harvest would impart*
> *The incorruptible beauty Men desire.*
> *But because gold cannot be worked when pure,*
> *Man added dirt and greed and jealousy,*
> *Violent obsession and the lust for more*
> *And more and more and more and more and more.*
> *And when they'd harvested the golden hoard,*
> *They made new images of golden beasts,*
> *And fell upon their faces and adored:*
> *Forgot the old gods, the old religion and its priests.*

Valmir was filled with a sudden surge of excitement and emotion. To think that there was another poet who thought as he thought, who could see beyond the dazzling temptation of the gold in the street to the evil ahead! But who?

'It's good, isn't it?' said a familiar voice behind him, full of proprietorial pride. It was Inez.

'*You* wrote it?'

'Of course not. I don't even understand it, quite. But it's very beautiful, isn't it? Don't you think the handwriting's beautiful?'

Valmir's joy trickled away like gravel through a *caixa*. 'Your priest wrote it, did he?'

'It's his handwriting. I recognize it,' said Inez proudly. 'Are you going to hang one up too?'

Inside his pocket, Valmir screwed up his poem. How could a militant communist sully his verse by letting it hang next to the work of a Catholic priest, a deceiver of the working classes? Only now, as he looked about unsuccessfully for the town's missing litter bin, did he notice that the square had been hung with brand new bunting in preparation for Independence Day. His poem, Ignatius's poem, any poem would be lost, in any case—two white oddities among the red and green and blue pennons.

On the football pitch, after the game was over, a little circus began to set up. No one had invited it. No one knew from where it had come or how long it would stay. But while boys like Maro hopped about on the touchlines, changing their football shorts for crisp new denims, their boots for trainers, they watched it rising up—almost magically—out of the ground.

There was a cage with a sickly capybara pacing listlessly up and down inside. There were jugglers pitching silver clubs into the air, then running out from under them as they rained down again like wayward warheads. There was a woman who had been a pretty girl once and still wore the same costume of red sequins as then, along with a new expression of pain because it was so tight. There was a small Indian boy with a pony tail of glossy hair who bit his lip as he walked a tightrope two metres off the ground—walked and walked and walked it, because he had learned nothing more ambitious. There was a pair of clowns, too, their face-paint trickling down in the damp heat like tears, assaulting one another with real malice and no humour. Betweentimes they touted tickets, balloons, tinsel wands, and Polaroid instant pictures of themselves holding screaming toddlers close up to their grotesque faces.

The lady in red sequins climbed a rope ladder while her husband wrestled a suspiciously limp jacara snake which he finally thrust away into a property basket. Then she hung by her teeth from a silver pulley which winched her high into the evening air.

It was the very first circus either Inez or Maro had witnessed. Brother and sister spotted each other from opposite sides of the field, and Inez felt uneasy, as if she should not be there; as if, having set her face against the gold, she ought to turn her back on the trappings it brought to town. Like this. But somehow she could not tear herself away. She cheered up when she caught a glimpse of Father Ignatius among the crowds: his very presence she took for permission to be there herself. Maro was looking smug. His expression said: you see what gold gets you? Fun, sophistication, glamour, electricity; football in place of school; circuses and rock music; acrobats and oddities.

Beside him stood Enoque, his mouth ajar, one hand over one eye the better to focus. All his life he had spent in the wild places—Amazonian jungle, upland Colombia, the riverbanks of Guyana. Such civilization as this had passed him by all his life. 'Isn't it magnificent,' he breathed in awe, as the travelling spot chased and hovered uncertainly over the glittering red figure suspended by her teeth from the sky. 'Such magnificent *teeth*!' whispered Enoque.

Father Ignatius watched the da Souza baby toddling through the legs of the watching crowd, collecting the razor-edged ring-pulls from a hundred drinks cans. A clown with a camera swept it up brutally, and his fellow clown snapped the picture, then looked around for a purchaser. 'Your kid?' he said to the priest.

'Well, it's not *yours*,' said Ignatius, snatching the crying child to his chest.

Those magnificent teeth meanwhile continued to clench the sky-hook with the ferocious determination of a piranha up at the surface of the dark Amazon. She spun and spun and spun.

The *pium* flies, deserting the late light of the evening river, moved elsewhere: the bright, coloured air in front of the TV set, the bright snaking light of the *movimentado* sign outside Tony's. But mostly they converged on the cone of white light illuminating the lady in red, as she twirled like a satellite high above the football pitch. The *pium* fly is small, but its bite is also magnificent. The lady acrobat gave a sharp cry of pain, catastrophically opening her lips. She fell like a red meteorite, and bruised the close-cut turf of Vazia FC.

But Enoque went on gazing up at the cone of light—that sugar cornet of light suddenly emptied of its strawberry ice. He went on gazing at the silver pulley twirling like a crescent moon. 'What magnificent teeth!' he said once more. And he was perfectly right. For the acrobat's reinforced dentures continued to smile radiantly down on Serra Vazia, like a beneficent, almost invisible god.

5

REBAIXAMENTO

(The deepening of a *barranco*)

The *pium* flies are drawn to sunlit places. Small, black, vicious flies, they blight the river's sweetest places. First the sunlight, then the flies come swarming in in a horrible infestation. That is how it was in Serra Vazia. Just as Father Ignatius and Valmir had said it would be. First the sunlight. Next the infestation.

After the circus came the jolly coffee sellers, serving thick black coffee out of vacuum flasks to parched *garimpeiros*. Then there were the street vendors selling duck stew, *maniçoba*, and a delicious mixture of fried beans, shrimps, and hot pepper called *acarajé*. Every sight and savour added to the delights of living in a revitalized township. Next there were the estate agents, roaming the deserted areas of run-down housing, trying to track down ownership so as to rent shelter at outrageous prices to the never-ending stream of newcomers.

Soldiers, truck drivers, bus drivers, factory workers, bank clerks, shop assistants, students, farmers, and lumberjacks were deciding daily that their only hope of riches lay in throwing up their jobs and trekking to Serra Vazia—the gold at the end of the rainbow. A party of military police came and arrested all the men off one *barranco* for being absent-without-leave from their army barracks. The hole was instantly taken over by yet another hopeful—this time the driver of the trucks which brought Mr da Souza's supplies twice a week from Marabá. He and his four brothers were *garimpeiros* now, they said, and proved quite deaf to da Souza's entreaties. 'But how am I supposed to get my supplies? Who's going to be driving the

41

truck?' There was no truck. The truck had been sold to buy *moinho* and *chupadeira*.

And all of a sudden, that was the least of da Souza's problems. For there was less that needed shipping, fewer orders, less custom at the store. Strange, in such times of plenty?

Another arrival. The Dealer came in by one of the rickety little aeroplanes called *teco-tecos*, with a briefcase full of money. He took a bedroom at the Hotel d'Ouro and sat on his bed, in leather shoes and an Italian suit, giving audience to the successful, to the *bamburrados*, to those who had struck it rich—or at least found something. A small portable radio on his bedside table was tuned to a station which broadcast, throughout the day, the current value of gold, solely for the information of men like himself. Apart from the briefcase, the only tool of his trade was a pair of precision scales, for the accurate weighing of pure gold. He would not be hurried in his calculations, either, so that a queue often formed outside his bedroom that extended half-way down the stairs. When his briefcase was empty, he went downstairs to deposit his gold in the hotel safe-deposit box and withdraw further cash from the Banco do Brasil down the street. Otherwise he never left his room, but sent small boys to buy him palm-heart *empadas* from the *lanchonete* on the square. Always an *empada* pasty. Always palm-heart—never shrimp or meat.

His slowness was in keeping with his physical characteristics, and did not lessen his overall likeness to a giant anteater. With his long nose and long top lip puckering out beneath it he appeared to be concealing a huge, curled, sticky tongue, its veiny underside pushing through his open lips as he counted out cruzeiro notes. Returning from his wearisome expeditions to the safe-deposit box downstairs, he rolled up the stairs, hunching his shoulders—like an anteater walking up a tree—and even the Italianate shoes could not disguise the fact that he, too, walked on the outsides of his feet. The Dealer brought

42

with him bodyguards lumpy with weaponry, as cacti are lumpy with pears. They slept on the floor at night and stood against the walls during the day, as if any sudden or jerky movement on their part might dislodge the anteater from its tree. They took it in turns to go and buy their own lunches, and it was then that Maro liked to follow them. He was curious to see whether they would snatch out a gun and shoot anybody down in cold blood. Like in the gangster movies.

This was how Maro came to discover the reason for the fall-off in business at his father's store. For the bodyguards did not buy lunch at the *lanchonete*. They went to the new *cantina* parked on Obidos Street.

It parked on an island of solid ground while all around the street decayed into trench warfare. With too many miners to work the Main Street, the newcomers inevitably struck off down the side streets, the parallel streets, the alleyways, the storm drain, the deserted rubber factory yards. And when they stopped work now, they too went to the *cantina*—a converted motorhome perched amid the squalor. It was not much to look at, but stowed within its extraordinary elastic walls was all a *garimpeiro* could need: rice, beans, manioc flour, cigarettes, medicines, batteries, soap, tinned meat and fruit, cooking oil, and diesel.

To and fro the van travelled in the small hours of the night, its roofline picked out in multi-coloured lightbulbs, its headlamps feeling the way between the pits like the white barbels of a catfish. Its klaxon played 'America! America!' By morning it was back in place again, and its tender was full of gasoline and diesel to power the hungry *moinhos* and pumps, its shelves restocked with everything a *garimpeiro* could desire.

The mood around da Souza's dinner table became suddenly sombre. Each time their father opened his mouth, Maro and Inez knew it would be to speak ill of *La Cantina*. 'Credit. He sells everything on credit! How can I compete with a man who sells everything on credit?'

Mrs da Souza banged the pots together in angry solidarity, and cleared the table before anyone had finished eating. 'How can I get the stocks to compete with him? Can I put wheels on the store and drive off to town? Can I?' Mrs da Souza smacked The Baby for sieving the lumps out of its custard with the tea strainer. 'He's selling liquor. I know it. *Chope* beer and *cachaça*. He takes it from the Indians in part-payment. I'll get him for that. I'll close him down, you see if I don't.'

But whether the local policemen chose the wrong time for their inspections of the *cantina*, or whether they were bought off with a crate of sugar-cane rum, there was no prosecution. The *cantina* continued to trundle the night streets like a monstrous *carbunco* feeding off Serra Vazia's gold. On the dashboard, where others stood football mascots or religious statues, balanced a pair of precision scales just like those on the Dealer's bedside table. Not only did the *cantina*-man advance credit, he accepted payment in gold-dust.

Very little gold-dust found its way into Vazia's Drugstore after the arrival of the *cantina*. On the contrary, Mr da Souza had stocked up to the ceiling with goods which were not now selling. The supplier wanted paying, and Mr da Souza did not have the money to pay. When he went to the Bank Itau next door to withdraw his savings, he found its doors locked, its lights out. A small notice on the door said, 'CLOSED DUE TO STAFF SHORTAGES'. The bank clerks—even the bank manager—had joined the ranks of the *garimpeiros*. And Mr da Souza's savings were incarcerated in the bank.

He went to the Expresos bus garage in Obidos Street. To his way of thinking, only Gomez the bus driver could save him from the shame, the disaster, the horror of falling into debt, a thing he had never done, not even in the bad old times. He should have foreseen a difficulty as soon as he saw Gomez wearing his Expresos cap on back-to-front, with the peak down over his neck.

44

'My truck driver's gone mad,' said da Souza jovially, offering Gomez a cigar. 'He's turned *garimpeiro*! Doesn't seem interested in earning an honest wage any more. Thing is, I bought myself a load of stock when the rush began. Now that bastard *cantineiro* is taking all my trade. And the suppliers want paying for stuff I haven't sold! Be a mate and take some of it back for me? Back to Marabá?'

'Love to help,' said Gomez, 'but you see my problem.' Taking da Souza by one arm, as though supporting an old man out of church, Gomez led the storekeeper round to the back of the garage. There, alongside an inspection pit which had once allowed Gomez to grease his axles and inspect his tracking rods, the yellow Expresos bus stood rattling its tinny doors and belching black exhaust. Its bonnet was open to allow the engine to power Gomez's own mining machinery. All four wheels had been removed and elaborate home-made conveyor belts carried spade-loads of gravel on bizarre, apparently purposeless journeys around the bus station yard. The inspection pit had grown into a gaping opencast mine. 'Always fancied myself a bit of an inventor,' said Gomez proudly. 'Raised two ounces last week!'

Around da Souza the jungle closed in, closed ranks, trees jostling together like thugs in an alleyway, blocking off all means of escape. For the first time in his life, he felt trapped in his own town, unable to leave, unable to summon help. At dinner that night he announced, 'I have a thing to say, and you, Inez, you hold your tongue. And you, Valmir— remember you are a guest in this house.' The family's mouths snapped shut in alarm. The bright new lamp on the table cast no shadows, and yet there appeared once more to be bands of darkness across their mother's face. 'I believe it is time to dig for gold,' said da Souza. 'If we're to get ourselves out of this present . . . temporary . . . difficulty . . . out of this slight setback in our luck. The store won't keep us, at the moment. So we must put in a little *extra* work . . . somewhere else. Pitch in. Like the rest.'

'Great!' cried Maro. 'Wait till I tell Enoque!'

'No!' cried Inez. 'Father Ignatius said . . .'

'Go to bed, Inez!' said her mother, and Inez removed herself from the table, pale-faced, looking like a martyr on the way to sainthood.

'Now it begins,' said Valmir darkly, and Mrs da Souza, standing behind him with a plume of chicory, broke it over his head.

That night, though Serra Vazia had learned to sleep through the eerie wail of drainage pumps and the strains of 'America! America!' the whole town woke up at the sound of a gunshot. No body was found in the morning, but then the whole town began to look like an open grave, and its ever-moving terraces of mud could have hidden anything. Who was to miss one stranger among a thousand? Soon afterwards, the gun-pedlars arrived on the street corners, openly selling arms to the *garimpeiros* to protect themselves, their *barrancos*, their takings. Perhaps the gun-pedlars fired that first shot, to guarantee good trade. Or perhaps the sugar-cane rum, now freely available everywhere but at da Souza's store, had enflamed a disagreement into a quarrel, a falling-out into a murder.

It was easier said than done—to join in the digging. By the time Mr and Mrs da Souza and Maro went out to sink a hole of their own, the streets in front of and behind their home and the alleyways to either side had all been excavated to a depth of three metres. Indian women and children slithered single-file on bare feet to and from the river, huge baskets of earth on their heads, to wash and pan in the moving water, for lack of expensive machinery. On the few remaining patches of flat ground—inside garages, in gardens, down cul-de-sacs, boys had been posted with nothing else to do all day than stake a claim and drive off rivals. Alfredo had found himself such a job. Too clumsy to be trusted on a *barranco*, he had been posted with a shotgun, in a narrow alleyway. And there he stood, feet apart, knees braced, cradling the gun as though it made him Lampião, the Bandit King. 'Clear off!' he bawled at Maro.

Maro laughed—took it for a joke—started to saunter into the alley. 'Better than school this, eh?' he said. It was a kind of password, a signal that he and Alfredo were on the same side.

Alfredo snapped his shotgun shut and fired—BANG!—over Maro's head, rocking back on his heels at the recoil. Maro too rocked back on his heels. He could feel his open mouth letting in the hot breeze and the taste of cordite, could feel his hair standing up in the nape of his neck. This was Alfredo, the boy he had sat next to in class! 'Word is, you're looking for a patch to dig,' said Alfredo, pointing the gun directly at Maro's body. 'Well, you can't have this one! I'm guarding this one!'

It was a patch of dirt littered with old tins and broken bottles, smelling of cats. Someone had scrawled on the fence behind Alfredo's head, '*Senhora Ferretti loves Luciano Pavarotti*'.

'You're mad,' said Maro and fled.

Down at the river, the simple recreational pastime of slopping gravel about in panning bowls had been ousted—driven downstream and up. Technology had taken over. Apart from the countless hoses sucking water up to the pumps in town, criss-crossing and overheaped like snakes mating in a pit, out there in the centre of the river were four *balsa* rafts tethered to mooring posts. A *chupadeira* was mounted on each, its guzzling snout reaching over the side into the silt of the riverbed. All four were silent.

The sheer silence pacified Maro, slowed his racing pulse. If there was no room left on the street, there was always the river—that ever-changing passage of water belonging to no one, made eternally new by the rains in the great mountains. He liked the idea of a *balsa*. It had more romance than a hole in the ground. The sky was always brighter over the river.

Once, Valmir had told him, during the Seventies Gold Rush, every tree had been felled, every blade of grass washed away, the whole river emptied of fish, the banks churned into a soupy slurry by one-hundred-thousand feet. But after the mountain failed, new soil had washed downstream, clung to the rocks, grass had seeded itself in the soil; from somewhere fish had found their way back, and birds rediscovered the sappy little trees which planted themselves along the watermargin. The river had the power to make itself new again. It could be relied on to renew the da Souzas' good luck.

An Indian boy equipped with nothing much more than a face mask suddenly burst through the river's shining surface, shaking the water out of his long dark hair and jerking his thumb downwards, though it was not clear for whom the signal was meant.

Maro could do whatever that boy could do. He could swim like a fish. He was not much taken with the idea of the piranha, the electric catfish, the half-metre parajas with teeth like porcupine spines. But there would be turtles, too, and scarlet ibis reflected in the dark green water, bright million-fish, inias as big as dolphins, and glowing neon tetras. Yes, this was where he would set about making his father rich, finding fortunes of gold washed down from God-knows-where over white rapids and the scales of green crocodiles.

He caught sight of his sister's friend, Mundicarmo, running up and down the far bank, her plaits twisting round her like the long liana vines that dangled and tangled round the riverside trees. Not in school? Ah yes, he remembered why. Her brother Amilcar had come home from the Azores on a visit. That meant only Inez was left in the classroom now, brow-to-brow with the dreaded

Senhora Ferretti. He snickered at the thought and waved across the river at Mundicarmo, but she did not see him.

He stripped off to his shorts and plunged into the water. If he was to be a *mergulhador*, this was the perfect opportunity to see what the work entailed. Diving into the dark green warmth of the Xingu river was soporific, dreamlike. Though the sweat between his shoulderblades was washed away, the currents were so warm that he sweated afresh. The acidic water stung his eyes as he looked around him at the kingdom he was about to conquer: the shoals of million-fish, the clouds of green plankton blotting out the sky. The legs of the Indian boy thrashed by overhead, a storm of green bubbles. The base of the *balsa* had already grown long strands of greenery like some of his mother's hanging baskets. Maro surfaced for air.

On the bank, Mundicarmo pointed all her fingers at him and screamed hysterically, '*There he is! I knew he was all right! Didn't I tell you? Didn't I say? Amilcar! Amilcar! Amilcar!*'

What did she mean? Maro dived down again, sweating a little more all of a sudden. He decided to time how long he could stand on the bottom of the river searching for gold. The river pushed at him, pushed, pushed, pushed like an impatient bully in a queue. To keep upright, he had to take a step or two or three or four. He did not want to. Liana—those ropelike vines that smother every tree—hung down among the tree-roots and drifted out like green squid through the inky water. To keep from being swept into their tendrils, Maro struck out for the surface, but the current still carried him, face-forward, towards the treacherous tangle of floating vines. Half-way towards the emerald-green sky of algae, he met Mundicarmo's brother. Their hands brushed in the limpest of handshakes. Amilcar's legs had obviously become entangled in the knotting liana, and there, like a victim of the green-haired Medusa, he looked out through the window of his flooded face-mask, still wearing a look of astonishment. That the river should get the better of him! That his manly strength should fail him!

By the time Maro had swum back to the bank where he had left his clothes, a little sorrowful crowd had gathered at the news of Amilcar's drowning. Mundicarmo was still shrieking on the opposite bank that she had seen him—spotted him alive and waving on the surface—but she was not believed.

Mrs da Souza was among the little knot of grieving women. She rushed at Maro with such a look on her face that he tried to duck out of reach. But she caught him unerringly round the neck with one muscular arm. One twist, he thought, and she would snap off his head, as she had once deadheaded the orchids in their boxes. But she only drew his head against her bony ribs and hugged him so tightly to her that he could feel her heart banging.

'I thought we could get a raft . . .' he began to say.

'Then think again,' she said very quietly, her lips pressed to the crown of his head. 'Just think again, my boy.'

Suddenly the generators on the rafts started up. Mining from *balsas* was not a silent process, after all: they had simply called a halt while the search went on for Amilcar. Unable to stand idle for another unprofitable moment, they burst into life one by one, whining and grating and clattering with a cacophony that dislodged all the parakeets and tanager birds from their roosts like a palette of paints being kicked into the sky.

Enoque came to the family's rescue. He and Honorio employed Mr da Souza outside his own front door. They let him work as a *diarista*—a paid hand earning two dollars a day for his labour. Mrs da Souza and Inez and Valmir ran the store, while outside in the street da Souza and Maro shovelled gravel to feed the *chupadeira*, like the slaves of some eternally hungry monster.

That was what most of the miners proved to be—paid labourers with no more chance of becoming rich than they had had when they emptied rubbish carts in Marabá or chipped stone on the face of Manaus Cathedral. They came to Vazia, used up their meagre resources, and became *diaristas* in a luckier man's *barranco*. It accounted for the lack of millionaires. Serra Vazia had gold—and yet no one seemed to be getting rich.

6

BETRAYAL

Needless to say, Inez did not approve of her father's new employment. Separated from the influence of her schoolfriends, she became more and more earnest in her opinions, more and more fanatical in her passions. She went to Mass four times a week, gazing up at Father Ignatius like a little bulge-eyed tree frog, collecting every word that fell from his mouth. She collected his words as The Baby collected the rusty nails dropping from the drugstore shingles. (The vibrations of machinery shook them loose.) At school, she listened with sober attention to her lessons. The nasty word 'gold' was never mentioned. El Dorado was no longer considered an 'acceptable' subject for the Independence Day parade, and was replaced with 'Flowers of the Forest'.

In fact, a kind of alliance grew up between Inez and Senhora Ferretti. They never referred to the disappearance of the rest of the class, to the progress of the digging, to the size of finds, to the death of Amilcar. Such things were tacitly understood to be not nice, in poor taste, best ignored. So in craft lessons, Inez painted newspaper in bright colours, and cut out circles to make flowers of the forest. The cheap newspaper ink was re-animated by the wet paintbrush and turned everything greyish. Beside her, La Senhora stapled pleats and folds into the paper and threaded her own hair pins through the flowerheads to make bendy stems.

For lack of a friend to confide in, Inez even said one day, as she painted, that she thought Father Ignatius was 'probably the most wonderful man in all Brazil'.

'I hope you won't always think so,' said La Senhora drily, then went on bending hairgrips.

On the morning of Independence Day, even though it was a public holiday, Senhora Ferretti turned up at the schoolhouse to pin the handmade flowers to Inez's dress. 'I thought you said your mother would put one of her orchids in your hair.'

'They're gone.'

'Her orchids?'

'Last night. The *garimps* ripped up the boardwalk to dig underneath it. All round the store. Now you step right out of the door into the pit. Mama's flowers went with the boardwalk.'

Senhora Ferretti said nothing in response. How could she without breaking their code of silence. 'You look lovely anyway, my dear,' she said instead, inflating her throat and chest like a pouter pigeon. 'Now remember to *feel* beautiful. You represent the school.' She laid across Inez's shoulder the strap of the school tape-recorder. It was an immensely heavy privilege to bear. The tape inside it played Tchaikovsky's 'Waltz of the Flowers'—a little slowly, owing to the age of the batteries.

Then La Senhora pinned another newspaper orchid into Inez's hair and opened the door very wide to let her pass through in her handicraft finery. Still neither of them knew whether the traditional parade would even be taking place—whether crowds would be waiting in the town square or whether the public holiday would pass unobserved, washed away in a sea of greed and mud.

But the holiday was never at risk. The *Banco de Brasil* stayed shut, so the Dealer could not open for business at the Hotel d'Ouro. The *cantina* could get no supplies of petrol or diesel. The *moinhos* fell silent, the hoses sagged flat. The coffee vendors sang patriotic songs on the street corners, the square fluttered its bunting of coloured flags and little white poems, and the parade formed.

The circus performers had harnessed the capybara's cage to a small donkey. They balanced on the cage roof now, parping horns and swinging rattles. The lady in red, her leg in plaster, was obliged to watch from the sidelines, not daring to smile for lack of her teeth. But the same clowns thrust the same merchandise at the same parents, who bought it for their children today, because public holidays always make people happy and sentimental.

A farm truck, decorated with plasterboard to look like a birthday cake, burst its icing, and out leapt five, six, seven young women, each swathed in a national flag. When they unfurled the flags and raised them on poles, they were wearing nothing underneath but the briefest costumes made of gold lamé. It was ten in the morning and they were already slightly drunk. The *garimpeiros* boggled with bloodshot eyes, then whistled and stamped and roared. The girls bent over to throw artificial flowers between their legs, teetering on high heels. Standing in the shade of the public television, Inez glimpsed her mother sweeping up The Baby, covering Maro's eyes, and hustling them both away from such lewd and wicked sights.

With Main Street dug up, there was nowhere for the 'parade' to progress, so it circled the square in an aimless, dizzying coil, trapping the spectators in the centre like rabbits in a dwindling field of corn. Inez, festooned in scraps of coloured newspaper, was caught up in the circle of tawdriness, and carried round the square, against her will. She saw Senhora Ferretti turn away and hide her eyes. Banging on Inez's hip, tinny Tchaikovsky waltzed slower and slower. La Senhora had told her to dance to the music, her arms outstretched, her feet thinking beautiful thoughts. But Inez could not summon any beautiful thoughts to mind or foot while surrounded by so much ugliness. She could hear only the clowns' horns quacking derisively, the donkey braying, the naked women singing rude versions of the National Anthem in half-remembered drunken snatches. She wanted to cry. She wanted the ground to open up and swallow her. She wanted the ground to swallow the whole town of Serra Vazia and with it her humiliation.

She, like the tape recorder, had just ground to a halt when she saw Enoque Furtado coming towards her in fits and starts, the toes of his boots catching in the dirt here and there, making him stumble. He had gathered up all the broken flowerheads he could find among the ruins of Mrs da Souza's tub-garden and stuffed them into his hat. Orchids and cabbage leaves, nettles and geraniums, he laid them in her arms in the oil-stained cradle of his sweaty hat. 'For the most beautiful girl in the parade,' he said, snorting through his blocked sinuses, covering one eye with his hand. His pet tayra ran round and round his neck, alarmed by the football rattles in the crowd, and came to rest sitting on top of his head.

'Don't you remember what happened in *Treasure of the Sierra Madre*?' begged Father Ignatius of his Sunday congregation. 'Don't you recall how things turned out in *King Solomon's Mines*?' He had stopped citing the Bible and resorted to the cinema in his one-man crusade against the gold-fever. He knew the *garimps* thought of themselves as devout Catholics: their dug-outs were festooned with holy medals and postcards of the Virgin. So the Father reminded them of movies instead of God's word—movies in which the lust for gold led to nothing but sorry death, to gold-dust trickling away through the clawing fingers of dying men. 'Think of Ben Gunn in *Treasure Island*!' The congregation stirred resentfully.

Inez da Souza did not remember *Treasure of the Sierra Madre*, and she thought that *King Solomon's Mines* must feature somewhere in the Bible. But she knew, with a peaceful inner certainty, that the *garimps* were wrong and Father Ignatius was right. The gold-mining was evil. It had killed Mundicarmo's brother, brought gangsters into town, ruined her father's store, blighted Alfredo and Carlos and Maro's chances of an education. Though no one but she believed the priest, soon they would all learn better. The boys would come back snivelling, cap-in-hand to the schoolhouse. But Senhora Ferretti would turn them away, like Noah closing the doors of the ark. Inez smiled a smile of grim satisfaction.

Inside her pocket she fingered the folds of Father Ignatius's ballad, taken down from its string in the square where it had hung unappreciated. She would take better care of it, treat it with reverence. That morning, before church, she had spent a great deal of time looking in the mirror. You might have thought she was trying to make herself look pretty, but she was really only looking to see what Suffering had done to her face. Her ordeal in the town square, her refusal to dance to the new music, her refusal to watch TV in colour, her hours spent praying in Santa Barbara Church . . . it had *aged* her, no doubt about it. From a child into a woman, almost. She was sure Father Ignatius would notice.

'Stop admiring yourself in the mirror and get The Baby ready, can't you?' her mother had said. But her mother did not understand. Only the likes of Father Ignatius and the cultured, refined Senhora Ferretti understood: Inez was no longer a child. At the church door she held out her hand, as the adults did, to shake hands with Ignatius. He shook it, too. Such a firm, sure grip.

The congregation bunched together on the church steps for a moment, like passengers on a harbour wharf, looking out to sea. Each family had to navigate a route home now through shoals of mud, machinery, and hardcore. The side-streets were all under excavation, the boardwalks ripped up and used to keep the steep sides of trenches from crumbling.

To reach the church, the da Souzas, dressed in their Sunday best, had had to negotiate a series of bending planks and stepping stones made from crates and oil cans. During the church service, the *garimpeiros* outside inevitably found another use for the crates or the planks—and a new route home had to be worked out.

'How deep will they go before they stop?' Mrs da Souza asked her husband, sponging the mud off her stockings in the kitchen. Mr da Souza shrugged. He was only one of the *diaristas*. Nobody told him anything.

'I'll ask Enoque,' said Maro. 'Enoque will know.'

'Oh, shut up! Enoque knows nothing!' said Inez with contempt. 'He's nothing but a *caboclo*. A hick. A bumpkin.'

'Enoque knows everything!' retorted Maro hotly. 'Enoque learned from the Indians how to tame that tayra of his. Enoque used to mine diamonds! Enoque can shoot poisonous darts and hit a monkey at fifty paces! Enoque used to play football for Porto Nacional!'

'Now I know you're lying! He can't even walk straight in his boots!'

'Children. Children, please,' said Mr da Souza from underneath the clean washing piled on the hammock.

'Enoque has seen the Indian spirits!' Maro persisted.

'Then he's a heathen, too, and he'll burn in Hell for it!'

'*Children*!' moaned Mr da Souza. The music of *forró* dancing in the square drifted down the street, but since starting to dig, all their father wanted to do on a Sunday was sleep beneath the washing, undisturbed. Mrs da Souza stood in the doorway and listened to the music wistfully, wishfully.

Next morning, Inez set off across the plank bridges, arms outstretched for balance, towards school and her lonely pursuit of knowledge. The journey took so long that she was late. Finding the front door locked, she assumed La Senhora had been delayed, too. Fortunately, half of the school's back wall had been stolen for shoring-planks, so she was able to reach her desk and sit waiting.

There she sat, her fingers stroking the creases out of Father Ignatius's poetry. She had decided to show it to Senhora Ferretti who would appreciate it for the superb literature it was: who might even explain the bits Inez did not understand. But Senhora Ferretti did not come. All morning Inez sat and wondered why.

Was she too embarrassed by the humiliation of the Independence Day parade to face Inez over a school desk? Surely the humiliation had all belonged to Inez.

Was she too disgusted by the town that she had packed her bags and gone? No. Where would she go and how would she get there? The only traffic was *into* Vazia, not out of it.

Had she caught malaria, perhaps? It was rife among the *garimps*; and Valmir had said it was bound to spread to the townsfolk before long . . .

Had she been attacked by the low-life who lurked now on the window ledges of the alleyways drumming their heels on the wooden walls of the houses and begging from passers-by with a knife in one hand?

Or had she simply fallen into a *barranco* on the way to school, and hurt herself? Hers was not the figure to entrust to thin, sagging planks of wood. Inez ought to go and look for her. And yet she waited.

All morning she waited, until paper El Dorado, surprised by the new draughts from the gaping hole in the wall, suddenly flung himself face-down across Inez, showering her with sand and drawing-pins. His paper arms wrapped her round, his face pressed close against hers, coarse as sandpaper. She pushed the collage away in such a panic that El Dorado tore. It was surely an omen.

She did not even stay to repack her satchel, but ran out of the schoolhouse calling her teacher's name. She was terribly alarmed. Something dreadful had happened, if only she knew what. At the end of Obidos Street she passed her former classmate, Alfredo, sitting in an alleyway piled with sacks of slag from the *barrancos*. He had a shotgun over his knees. 'Have you seen La Senhora?' she asked him.

'What Senhora?'

'*Our* Senhora, of course! Senhora Ferretti! Have you seen her?'

58

'Who needs it?' His eyes trailed about in her general direction, but she was not at all sure he could see her, or knew who she was.

'Are you drunk, Alfredo Pessoa?'

'I'm the king of the castle,' said Alfredo, baring his teeth in an ape-like expression. 'I'm the cast of the kingle.' He dropped his gun and, in trying to catch hold of it, slithered down the pile of sacks and almost rolled into the five-metre hole beyond. The *garimps* in the hole swung at him with their spades.

'Have you seen Senhora Ferretti? The teacher lady?' Inez called down to the miners, but they only shrugged and indicated they could not hear her above the noise of their rock-crusher.

'Maro! Have you seen La Senhora?' she shouted across Main Street. Her brother looked up at the sound of his name, but by the time she had crossed over the elaborate maze of plank bridges, he had sloped away. Honorio Furtado emerged from the hole. 'Boy? Maro! Where'd he push off to, eh? First Enoque. Now him. Don't nobody do no work on a Monday these days?'

In the bottom of the trench, Mr da Souza shielded his eyes against the sun. 'Inez? Why aren't you in school?'

'I can't find Senhora Ferretti, Papa,' she called down. 'She didn't come to school this morning, and I can't find her!'

'The singing lady? Oh, I know where *she* is,' said Honorio, scrabbling up out of the pit. 'You come with me. I have to get my brother back from her in any case.'

'She's with *Enoque*?' She followed him disbelievingly. His weight and speed set the plank bridges ahead of her bowing and springing. Honorio led her towards the Hotel d'Ouro, but they did not need to complete the journey before Inez knew the whereabouts of Senhora Ferretti.

All the hotel's windows and blinds were shut against the cacophony of machine noise in the street, and yet La Senhora's voice still escaped between the shingles. It clambered out of the air-conditioning vents. It set the spider monkeys on the roof dancing as though the tiles were hot.

'*Ai! Ai! Samba!*
Ai! Ai! Samba!
It's the rhythm of the music in the street.
It's the rhythm of the dancing in your feet.
It's the swaying of a woman when she starts
The rhythm pulsing in her lover's heart . . .
Ai! Ai! Samba! . . .'

Inez followed Honorio through the hotel lobby. The whole of the downstairs had been turned into a recreation room. There were pool tables, table-football, and coin-in-the-slot machines with gaudy flashing lights darting and spiralling towards luminous dollar signs. A croupier in a bikini and a head-dress of rhea feathers was dealing cards to men in moleskin trousers, with hats like oil sumps. Their hands crouching on the table edge were black tarantulas. At another table a pair of white dice clattered against the end of a crap table. But no amount of noise confounded Senhora Ferretti.

Standing on a stage decorated to look like a palmy grotto, and holding a microphone as big as a bullrush, she wore an ancient satin dress seeded with black jet so that she shimmered like a geyser of crude oil each time she shook her gigantic hips. The dress was cut so low at the back and fitted so tightly that the flesh of her shoulders and hips brimmed over the restraining black binding—white, mottled, damp with sweat. A single spot of light impaled her to the stage like a pin impaling a live black beetle.

'*Ai! Ai! Samba!*
Ai! Ai! Samba!
So take me somewhere where the band is feeling hot
And take me somewhere where the cachaça is not.
Oh take me where the moon throws down its shiny light
But hides the dance of lovers out-of-sight . . .
Ai! Ai! Samba!
Ai! Ai! Samba!'

60

In front of her the *garimps*, freshly happy from visiting the Dealer, danced the samba with a mindless, careless abandon—men dancing with men, men dancing with their wives, men dancing with their children, men dancing with the hostesses hired by the hotel to wear swimming costumes and drink champagne at the customers' expense. Inez recognized some of the hostesses from the Independence Day parade: recognized the swimming costumes at least. They wore silver sandals with ten-centimetre heels, so that they towered over the little undernourished *garimps*. Great hanks of dyed golden hair dangled into the men's faces like tree creepers.

Standing there in knee-socks spattered with mud, her white school pinafore, her clean gingham frock, Inez stared at Senhora Ferretti with a hatred so intense that she believed the singer must feel it.

But the singer's eyes remained closed in the rhapsody of song:

'*Ai! Ai! Samba!*
Ai! Ai! Samba!'

Honorio, meanwhile, had threaded his way across the dance floor to a table hard up against the stage, where his brother sat drinking a *suco* and gazing up at La Senhora like a tourist admiring the Statue of Liberty. Inez could see his lips forming the words ' . . . wonderful, wonderful, marvellous . . .' as his brother levered him out of his chair. Enoque made a snatch at an arrangement of plastic flowers and, having only haphazard success, pulled out a plastic palm frond and threw it, by way of a tribute, at La Senhora's feet. Its sharp leaves scratched her ankles and she looked down as though it might be an insult.

' . . . spend your days watching the women . . .' Honorio was saying reproachfully, '. . . leave us to do all the work . . .' as he steered Enoque back across the dance floor. Enoque rocked his hips in time to the samba. The music washed his voice into fragments.

' . . . on my way to the church . . . heard it . . . couldn't

61

keep away . . . What a woman! What a voice!' Enoque samba'd to a halt in front of Inez. 'Isn't your teacher a *wonderful, wonderful* woman?—Hey! You go to church a lot, don't you? Maro said. Regular as a saint, he said. I was going there just now. To the church. To take this. But that priest . . . well. Not sure that priest cares for us *garimps*. Not sure he'd go for me dirtying up his church, sort of thing. Be a good girl. Take it there for me. To Santa Lucia. To Santa Lucia, yes?' He thrust something into her hand wrapped in a grubby handkerchief.

'I thought you worshipped the Indians' gods,' Inez said priggishly. 'Maro said . . .'

'So? Does it mean I don't got respect for the saints? God's my judge, I have! Never gave no one's gods no offence, me. Santa Lucia, you hear? She's the one in charge of eyes, isn't she? Lovely woman, your teacher! I'd listen to her three days sooner than two!'

A large party of *garimpeiros* leaving the hotel together swept Inez out on to the street, though she felt as if the music had rolled her there. She clung to the side of the building to keep from falling into The Pit, clutching Enoque's knotted handkerchief inside her fist. The thing inside it felt like a walnut or a stone. Perhaps it was a gold ingot thanking the saint for her help. But then surely it should be going to Santa Barbara, patron saint of miners.

Inez gave it some thought, but not much. Her heart was beating painfully fast and her cheeks burned with anticipation. She was about to see Father Ignatius—to pass something into his hands. She would be able to tell him about that traitor, that turncoat, that *loose woman*, Senhora Ferretti.

As she passed the end window of the hotel, the blind sprang up and spun noisily on its pole. Senhora Ferretti's face confronted Inez, caked with powder, the eyelids and sockets painted a dark shimmering blue. 'Better to sing for someone than lecture to no one!' she shouted through the glass. 'When you didn't come to school this morning—even you . . .'

'I was late!'

'When you didn't come I thought, better to sing for somebody than teach an empty room! People have to earn a living, you know? People have to eat!' The face pleaded for understanding, but at such close quarters the stage make-up was frighteningly grotesque. Inez reached a drainpipe and swung round the end of the hotel, out-of-sight of La Senhora, though the voice pursued her: 'How else could I ever get away from this place? That's what everyone wants, isn't it? To get away? To get out!'

Inez pressed on doggedly, clutching Enoque's handkerchief, picking her way over the slag heaps and planks to the church. She was very careful to keep her pinafore crisply pure. Her heart jumped now at the thought of meeting Father Ignatius one-to-one. She would cast all her sorrows and disappointments, her sense of betrayal, at his feet. She would probably cry. (In fact she was crying already, though she did not know it.) He would dry her tears and sympathize with the terrible loneliness of being Good.

She paused on the church steps to unknot Enoque's handkerchief. As the corners fell away, she squealed and dropped the contents. For Enoque's gift to Saint Lucia was a human eyeball.

In fact, Inez realized as it fell from her grasp that it was only the model of an eyeball. Enoque had carved it, using finest mahogany. It bounded off the steps, rolled down the side of a *barranco*, and lodged, with a squelch, close to the sucking nozzle of a *chupadeira*.

'Stop! Stop! Stop!' she shouted down at the men working below. Suddenly she knew what the eyeball was: an *ex voto*—a carving to show the saints what part of a sick man ailed him. The thought of Enoque's eyesight disappearing up the great slurping snout of the *chupadeira* made Inez jump and skid down the embankment on the heels of her shoes, filling them with mud and smearing the back of her pinafore and socks to a sewagey brown. 'Wait! Wait! Wait! I dropped something!'

The *garimp* holding the *chupadeira* drew it away, and Inez felt about in the mud for the little wooden lozenge until she found it. By the time she had managed to get out of the *barranco* and into the church, the mud hung from her hems in nasty clots, and plastered her hair to her cheeks. She was almost relieved that Father Ignatius appeared to be nowhere in the church. It would have been *dreadful* to have him see her looking like this.

A plaster Santa Lucia, neckless and squat, looked out over an empty nave. Inez placed the *ex voto* at the foot of the statue, wondering why she should do a *garimp* a favour. 'Gold is the root of all evil,' she recalled inaccurately, with a passionate sigh.

There was a peculiar draught blowing through the church. It drew the curtains of the vestry outwards. A door must be open somewhere other than the one she had come through. Inez let the draught carry her in the direction of the communion rail, until she saw that, beyond the reredos, the entrance of the crypt was open. An extension cable like a black snake crawled in at the corner of the opening.

Startling after the silence (and after thinking herself alone in the building) the unmistakable noise—*thump, crunch, hiss*—of a spade digging into gravel echoed through the church. Inez stood so still to listen that the mud in her hair dried. It crazed against her collar as she walked to the head of the crypt stairs and squatted down.

The extension cable coiled twice round a wooden joist then lit an inspection lamp which cast a spoked circle of light on the floor below. Several of the concrete paving slabs lining the crypt had been prised up and leaned against the walls. And in the centre of a shallow trench, wearing jeans and a T-shirt commemorating the Pope's visit to Rio, his hair yellower in the lamplight, Father Ignatius shovelled gravel into a waiting line of burlap sacks.

7

GRAFT

The look on Father Ignatius's face, when he caught sight of Inez sitting there on the brink of the vault was one she would always remember: every time she heard the story of Lucifer, the fallen angel, who sinned and was found out. 'And I thought you were so . . .'

For a long time that half-finished sentence was the only noise in the vault, its echo cannoning off the walls, roaring about in search of an ending. But there was no one word to describe all the things Inez had thought Father Ignatius to be. And here he was, grubbing for gold like all the rest.

'D'you think they'd've let it alone?' he shouted out at last. 'You think they won't think of this place in a week or two? You wait! There won't be one cellar left! There won't be a single floorboard! They'll dig it all up. Better I should, isn't it? Well, isn't it?'

As slowly as it takes the rain to percolate through a chalkstone hill, the tears welled up in Inez. When at last they came, they ran down a silent face, over her buckled lip, down her pointed chin. The first to drip into the vault fell to the floor but made no sound—only a dark round circle in the thick dust.

Ignatius saw it and stopped speaking, intimidated into silence by that single drop of water. He turned his back on her, squatted down, and stared at the wall with closed eyes, until he heard the scuff of her sandals down the nave overhead, the bang of the doors and the great silence of an empty church bearing down on him from above like the paving stones of Heaven on sinking foundations.

Ministério das Minas e Energia
Marabá

25th October

Honoured Sirs,
  I, a resident of Serra Vazia in the district of Para, write respectfully to draw your attention to the insufferable numbers of garimpeiros now mining, without restraint or consideration, the streets and thoroughfares of our town. Sirs, if something is not done, I fear the consequences of this wholly uncontrolled exploitation of the town's gold deposits. Where is the protection for the environment? Where is this mindless plunder to stop? The invasion of our neighbourhood, the desolation of our surroundings? Are we to see our own town dug up and carried piecemeal away? . . .

This letter of Valmir's ran to several pages, but most of those pages ended up in the waste-paper basket of the Federal Ministry of Mines and Energy. Just four words were picked out with an orange fluorescent highlight pen by the clerk who passed it on to his senior. 'Serra Vazia' and 'gold deposits'. The senior made a phone call to his friend at the *Companhia do Vale do Rio Xingu*—a mining company of which the federal government was a majority shareholder. If there were new gold deposits to be found anywhere in Brazil, it was essential that the state knew about them and enjoyed its fair share.

The *Companhia* asked questions of Military Intelligence. The MI notified the *Policia Militar*. Later that day, a police commander tilted his chair back against the wall and stared up at the green metal lampshade above him. Weren't there elections due in that part of the world?

'It's the first time I've ever been pleased to see the army,' said Valmir Zoderer several times over dinner. The great grin on his face made it plain he believed his letter—his very own letter—had saved Vazia from total destruction at the hands of the *garimps*. Perhaps, after all, the end of civilization was not at hand. The army had moved in to oversee the local elections and to issue just a *very few* licences to mine in Vazia Town.

True, it had sent a shiver of horror through the town when they came. There was a blast of air from overhead, like the breath of God. Their hats blew off, the mud around their feet blew into soft brown peaks like chocolate icing. The carpet oddments under their *caixas* flapped frayed edges, as a giant twin-rotor helicopter descended out of an equally metallic sky and hovered so low over Main Street that it almost shut out the sun. With infinite slowness it moved towards the only remaining area of undug land—the graveyard. Suddenly it was disgorging military police: they overran the square and formed a cordon around the town which made it hold its breath and freeze in abject terror. Then somewhere a megaphone coughed and somewhere—it was not plain from where—a disembodied voice declared, 'Let's get one thing straight, you *peãos*, you *brabos*. I'm here to put some law'n order into this place, and I'm not standing for no opp'zishun!' The *garimpeiros* went on looking up to heaven, like the shepherds visited by angels on Christmas night.

'We's here, by order of the Fed'ral Gov'ment, to purr-vent a breach of peace. All firearms to be s'rendered twuss. All illegal goods to be s'rendered twuss. *To wit*: any drugs, licker, 'fensive whipons, gambling deevices, transmittin' tel'phones or raydyas. Henceforthwith no minin' workin' to be done by no one without no 'ficial licence to op'rate within the precinx and s'rounds of this joorsdickshun. Let's us get some order back in this swamp, yeah, you flea-bitten *brabos*?'

With the dying *wha-wha-wha* of the helicopter rotor

blades, a silence fell over Vazia thicker than Christmas snow. No one could dig, since no one had a licence to dig. There was a kind of panic all along the *barrancos*. Where to go for these licences? Who needed to be bribed and how much? But it was a whispered panic in among the silent machinery. Mothers came and stood on their thresholds, smiling at the thought of renewed Law and Order.

The *garimpeiros* withdrew, like whipped dogs, licking their wounds, muttering at the interruption to their work, but sitting, ears pricked, at a distance, listening for news. Nothing ever stands still for long. Soon word would come of licences and how to get them. Serra Vazia waited on the blocks.

But in those few quiet days, an eerie stillness hung over the streets penetrated only by the voice of Senhora Ferretti in the Hotel d'Ouro entertaining the police officers to a selection of light operetta and samba music. Cats walked the planks bridging the pits, as well as the lone figure of schoolboy Alfredo Pessoa. Introduced to cane liquor by a *lanchonete* near his alleyway, Alfredo had quickly formed a craving for it so strong that he criss-crossed the *barrancos* knocking on the plank shops and house walls asking everyone where he could get something to 'make him happy'. He needed, he said, to be made happy again.

Raising his glass of mineral water to propose a toast, Valmir stood up gleefully. But out of the corner of his eye, he saw Mr da Souza wave a hesitant finger at him and shake his head, glancing his eyes sideways in the direction of Inez. Valmir saw that the child was weeping—silently, copiously—her shoulders rising and falling a little with the exertion, but every morsel of her strength given over to concealing her unhappiness. It had taken several days for the storm to break, but here it was, a monsoon of tears. The whole table stared at her, but her eyes were so tightly closed that she did not see them. Remarkable that tears should escape so freely through such tightly sealed lids. Valmir sat down again.

Even Maro knew better than to ask why his sister was crying. There was the feeling in the room that her sadness went deep—deep as the pit outside the door—and that no one there would know how to bridge it.

Just then a fist rapped on the window, and Enoque's face appeared, low down, in the bottom-most pane. Because there was no boardwalk left to stand on, he was clinging to the sill by his fingertips. His pet tayra ran excitedly from shoulder to shoulder over the top of his head, then wrapped itself around his throat in a furry collar. Maro rushed to open the window, being careful not to dislodge him.

'Come quick!' said the miner. 'Have you seen the queue at the d'Ouro? Come quick! It's first come, first served!'

Climbing out of the window, Maro could see that a queue, starting somewhere inside the Hotel d'Ouro, stretched out of its doors and right down Main Street. It snaked this way and that, balancing on overloaded planks, clinging to the muddy sides of the *barrancos*, squabbling and scrapping over who had got there first. The men in the line looked like refugees queuing to board the last ship out of a war-zone, their shoulders rounded, their heads thrust towards their only hope of survival.

Licences to dig were being issued at the Hotel d'Ouro. The man in the Cantina said a licence would be issued to every man who registered to vote in the forthcoming election. And to register, one had to go to the Hotel d'Ouro. 'Quick!' Enoque urged. 'We must get in the queue! We must register!'

Just then, came a blow on the door that buckled the insect screen and broke the glass panel of the door inside. It was so loud, so alarming, that Enoque lost his grip and slithered out of sight. A squad of armed soldiers struggled to push their way, two at a time, through the door, crushing the shards of glass to dust beneath metal-studded boots.

They turned over the dining table, broke a row of bottles by sweeping them off a shelf, and felled a pyramid of baked-bean cans. They threw open all the cupboards, pulled every drawer off its runners and tipped it upside down on the floor.

'Stop! *Stop! Please!* What is this? You're making some mistake!' protested Mr da Souza, while Valmir flattened himself against the wall as if he might pass for wallpaper. They pushed past him to the stairs and, up in the bedrooms, pulled all the bedding on to the floor, then broke all the lightbulbs. The listening family could hear the spines of books being systematically broken: it sounded like the killing of small animals.

Outside the window, Maro crouched alongside Enoque in the bottom of the pit. 'What do they want?' he whispered, tears pricking at the back of his eyes.

'Someone's shopped your Dadda, that's what,' said Enoque. 'Some bastard snitched on him to the military.'

'But he's done nothing!'

'You think that makes a difference somehow? A man makes enemies, a man's got to watch out.'

'Dad hasn't got enemies!'

'A man in trade, he always got enemies. It's that *cantiniero* after shutting down the shop. Fix your Dadda good if he can.'

'Not before I fix him!' Maro picked up a chunk of wood and stood up, his chest thrown out, his cheeks fat with the sheer size of his vengeance. Enoque snatched hold of him by the seat of the pants and pulled him back down into hiding. 'You wanna help your Dadda, you make sure them soldiers don't find nothing they's looking for.'

'Please explain,' Mrs da Souza was saying to the most high-ranking officer, in her sharpest, most high-ranking tones.

'Information's been received that you're selling liquor, in contravention of the emergency powers.'

71

'Liquor?' cried Inez.

But her father did not. He simply exchanged with his wife a look of weary despair and said, 'Information received? You mean the *cantiniero* has fixed me.'

The soldiers had been told precisely where to look, for after a token, destructive search of the store, they went outside and began looking under the house. The digging in the street had started to undermine the walls themselves, so that there was a hollow cavity all around the base of the building. Plainly Mr da Souza's rival in trade had told the military to look for a case of *cachaça* under the house. (It would be easy enough for him to plant one there).

But though the soldiers looked and looked, with increasing desperation, they could find no case of illegal liquor, no incriminating substance for which to close down the store. 'Sold it already, have you?' sneered the officer-in-charge. 'Well, so you got lucky. We'll get you next time, you *****, don't think we won't.' The troops withdrew, helping themselves to sweets off the shelf. They left behind them a smell of leather dubbin and violence, a feeling of having been punched, without the bruises to show for it. The whole family went and hung their heads out of the windows, to breathe in a different smell.

'I wonder why they didn't find anything,' said Mr da Souza.

'Because we made pretty damn sure they wou'n't,' said Enoque, grinning up from the bottom of the pit below. He and Maro wriggled out from under a canvas tarpaulin and Maro dragged out a crate, too. There was a tell-tale chink of glass bottles.

'Nice of the *cantiniero* to leave a case of *cachaça* outside your door, eh, Dad?'

The army raid had cost Enoque and the da Souzas a good place in the queue. They had to join the back of the line. Enoque darted his head continuously over the shoulder of the man in front, to see whether the queue was starting to move. He was deeply fearful that the licences

72

would run out before he could get one. 'Will you help me up the stairs, boy, will you?' he asked Maro repeatedly, with an agitation in his voice which upset the tayra and made it pluck up the strands of his shirt with long claws. 'My feet. Couldn't feel them too good this morning, when I got outa bed.'

The military police patrolled the queue, here and there and quite at random, pointing out a face they did not like and sending it to the end of the line. Now and then, with a noise like a thundercrack, a plank with several people balanced on it broke and precipitated them into the mud three metres below. A *garimpeiro* cursed a fat man for falling on top of his machinery.

At the back of his mind, Mr da Souza began to think differently of Valmir's letter to the Government. Supposing the licences were restricted to forty? To fifty? To sixty? There were at least ninety people ahead of them in the queue. Maro did not keep such thoughts to himself. 'This is all Valmir's fault. Him and his letters to the Government!'

Behind them, Valmir, too, climbed out of the store window. He had to join the queue to be sure of his vote. And though it would cost him agonies to vote for Honorio Furtado—a *garimpeiro*!—still nothing must stop Valmir the lifelong Socialist from writing his Socialist cross on the ballot paper.

And Inez, left behind at the wrecked dinner table, simply cried for reasons of her own.

Enoque need not have worried. The licences did not run out. The queue gradually dwindled and dwindled. They found themselves in the hotel lobby, on its stairs, in its upstairs corridor. They passed the open door of Room Number 13, where The Dealer sat on his bed beside a suitcase full of money. His little precision scales stood idle on the bedside table. He had nothing better to do than shine his leather shoes with toilet paper; little screwed up scraps were strewn round his feet. Until there were miners

73

licensed to dig for gold, there would be no more gold for him to buy.

In the room next door, the local Electoral Registrar sat at one table, guarded by a soldier with a sub-machine gun. There was, at another, an attractive woman officer who helped the illiterate *garimpeiros* to fill out the forms. She held their calloused hands while they made their marks of consent. Enoque made his mark so eagerly that the pen dug deep into the paper, and a great blot overspilled his name. 'Sorry, sorry, sorry,' he said.

The lady stroked his hand. 'Don't worry. That's just fine. Just take this to the Registrar and he'll put you on the Electoral Roll and give you your licence to mine. Don't forget though,' she crooned, 'if those dreadful Socialists get in, these licences won't be worth the paper they're printed on after tomorrow. These are issued by a *Democratic government* authority. So don't forget. If you want to go on digging after tomorrow, you'll have to *vote Democrat*, won't you?' And she gave a little girlish giggle.

'Oh, but I couldn't do that,' Enoque began to say. 'My brother's standing as the Sociali . . .'

Mr da Souza kicked him from behind, and jostled him out of the way, trying to keep him from saying the wrong thing. 'Don't hold up the queue! Make room for the next in line.' And as the storekeeper filled up the forms, and the pretty woman stroked his hand and said all the same things to him, Enoque stood by rubbing his leg, covering one eye and looking confused.

'. . . Don't forget, though, if those dreadful Socialists get in,' the woman crooned on in her lilting, routine voice, 'these licences won't be worth the paper they're printed on after tomorrow. So remember: if you want to go on digging after tomorrow, you'll have to vote Democrat, won't you, ha ha ha!' She beamed at each man, her jaw fixed in a vice of a smile. 'If the *Socialists* get in, all these licences will be immediately *null and void*. You must vote according to your beliefs, naturally, but . . .'

'I understand. I understand,' said each man hastily. 'I'll vote Democrat.'

'Good man!'

Later, Enoque gazed back up the hotel stairs, mourning his loss of understanding. Once, a month or so ago, he and his brother had been the *desbravadors* of Serra Vazia. Today, suddenly nobody was going to vote for Honorio in tomorrow's election! Such corruption made no sense to him. Gold was meant to make people rich, and yet here he was—the discoverer of a new gold reef and still perched on the very brink of ruin. Perhaps, after all, that clever college boy, Valmir, knew a thing or two. His head ached. His eyes were cloudy and would not work both together in his head.

That clever college boy Valmir took to his room and stared at the chaga beetles on the wall for two whole days. At the end of that time—after the election had been won in a landslide triumph by the ruling Democratic party—the military police left town.

No limit had been placed on the number of licences to dig. Everyone who wanted one, had been issued with one—and it had cost them no more than one cross on a ballot paper. Even Honorio had voted Democrat, knowing when to bend with the wind. After the soldiers and the Registrar and pretty woman left, a whole drawerful of the flimsy blue licences was found in Room 14 of the Hotel d'Ouro. The Registrar would have enfranchised the wistiti monkeys infesting the rooftops, if they had promised to vote Democrat.

For once in their lives, the *garimpeiros* had had something the Government wanted from them: their vote. Once that had been bought, the army melted away. The drug-dealers, gun-salesmen, and spivs reappeared on the street corners, and the Vazia Gold Strike took up where it had left off.

'*I* did it,' said Valmir to the chaga beetles on the wall. '*I* lost the election for the Socialists. Just by writing that stupid letter.' And he resolved never to write another word.

8

IN CHURCH

'I'm not going to church,' said Inez.

'Then you don't eat again in my house,' said her mother calmly. 'I don't feed heathens.'

Inez, defiant as she felt, refrained from saying that Mrs da Souza did not feed Christians either these days. The shop shelves fed them. The family ate tinned mandarin oranges and spam—ate anything which they did not need to buy elsewhere, for there were no profits to be had from the shop other than to eat it to emptiness, like a family of mice living in a cheese.

Thwarted in his plan to have Mr da Souza arrested for selling liquor, the *cantineiro* resorted to other ways of closing down the store. Under cover of night, paid thugs came and disturbed their peace with little random acts of vandalism: a brick through the window, a dead monkey tied to the insect screen. Youths came and loitered in the shop, flagrantly stealing; threatening and swearing at any customer who came through the door. The last of the customers quickly learned not to come. It was a terrible ordeal which Mrs da Souza likened to the persecution of the saints. But her husband could not help retorting that he had done nothing good enough to deserve it.

All the same, he too was shocked by his daughter's refusal to go to church. 'What's the matter with you? Time was, we couldn't keep you out of the place! Time was, you thought the sun shone out of that blond boy, that Father . . .'

'Don't speak that name in this house. I hate him. He's evil.'

Father and mother looked at each other over their tinned cling peaches. 'What did he do, dear?'

'He's a hypocrite and a liar and I hate him,' said Inez.

Valmir's spoon stopped on the way to his mouth and his socialist eyes glittered knowingly.

'Maro, go and practise for the match,' said Mrs da Souza all of a sudden, afraid that whatever Inez said might be unsuitable for Maro's ears. What scandalous thing could the Father possibly have done?

Maro clattered with his spoon, jabbing at peach slices like a cat pawing goldfish. He made no sign of moving. Inez began to cry again, trying to roll the tears back up her cheek with the side of one finger. 'Maro! Go and play football,' said his mother.

Suddenly Maro burst into tears as well. 'How can I? Don't you know anything? How can I? They dug it up! They dug up the goal mouths!'

'Well, can't you play sideways?' demanded Valmir, impatient to hear bad of the priest.

'They dug up the middle, too. *Barrancos* and toilets and tents. They've camped all over it, the *garimps*. There'll never be no football there ever again! Honorio would never've let it happen if he'd got elected! Enoque would never've let it happen!'

His mother corrected his grammar pedantically. 'There'll never be *any* football here . . .' but her voice tailed off with the momentousness of what she was saying. No football? No football in a Brazilian town full of men? Then the world had indeed fallen off its twin axes: Football and God. For Maro, the goalposts were down which had held up the sky. For Inez, the blond plaster saint who had propped up Heaven had somehow let it fall round her ears. Mrs da Souza felt strongly inclined to dive under the table to avoid the falling rubble of this universal collapse.

But instead she wriggled her feet into her painful Sunday shoes and clapped her hands imperiously. 'Everybody stop crying please! We are going to church! We are going to church because I say so, and the day I say we do not is the day my children may stay at home . . . Unless Inez can tell us just why our priest, our dear, good priest . . .!'

Inez saw no remedy but to tell: to lay the dreadful truth at their feet. 'He dug for gold, that's what. I found him. He was digging for gold. In the church! He's just like everyone else! Told everyone not to dig, didn't he? You heard him. It's the root of everything dreadful, that's what he said, isn't it? And all of a sudden he's got to have gold, got to get rich just like everyone else! Can't resist it. All of a sudden it's all right for *him*. He's different . . . he was digging for gold, I tell you! I found him!'

Valmir whistled softly under his breath. 'Let's go,' he said. 'Let's go to Mass.'

'*You?* Go to church?' said Mr da Souza. 'Today really is a day for surprises.'

'Let's go and confront him with it. Pitiful! Establishment hypocrite. All priests are the same. Money-mad hypocrites.'

Mrs da Souza sat down, her lace scarf already in place. '*Oh* no! We won't go in that case. I won't stand for a scene. I won't have you talking unbeliever's blasphemies in the church, Valmir Zoderer. Oh no. Oh no. Oh no.'

So in the end, they went without her: Inez and Maro and Valmir and Mr da Souza (who hoped to limit the damage).

The church was full. But the congregation was divided, by the centre aisle, into locals and strangers, into townsfolk and *garimpeiros*. And a gulf divided the two groups now wider than the ditch down Main Street.

The people of Vazia were confused. They needed guidance. Gold had been found under their town, and yet most was being dug up by strangers—outside their own front doors! Very few townsfolk were getting anything. Those who had staked claims to *barrancos* had been driven off by gangsters with six-guns—driven off their own street! And the town was becoming a nightmarish place overrun by criminals, spivs, and black-marketeers. Serra Vazia must be better off, for were there not signs of affluence all over town? So why did they feel so frightened and sad? They waited for Father Ignatius to reassure them. Perhaps he had been right all along to see gloom in the gold strike. They felt a strong inclination to huddle back to him like sheep to their shepherd. He would tell them now that the men digging the street were wicked and perverted, ungodly, and bound for Hell. That might just make the townspeople feel better.

On the other side of the aisle, the *garimpeiros* still just wanted the Mass to bring them good luck.

But when Father Ignatius reached the end of the Gospel reading and the point at which his homily should begin, he only stood silent in the pulpit as if he had forgotten his place in the service. The congregation leaned forwards a little, willing him on. His eyes were fixed on the pulpit rail, where his hands gripped the wood. He lifted each of his fingers in turn, as if counting them. He looked down at Inez da Souza, and she glared back at him with all the hatred of disappointed love. All through the service, he had been able to hear that atheistical student, Valmir Zoderer, chuckling and guffawing, calling it all mumbo jumbo. Father Ignatius coughed to clear his throat but said nothing, until at last he said, 'There is malaria in the tents on the football pitch.'

Aha! A judgement from God, eh? That's what he's going to tell us! thought the congregation.

'The funeral takes place today of Amilcar Lopez, who drowned, as you know . . . in the most tragic circumstances. The family requests your support in their time of sorrow.'

'*But I say he deserved all he got.' Is that what he's going to say?* wondered the congregation.

'His burial will be the last possible here in Serra Vazia . . . The graveyard, you see, is . . . full. That's to say, it's surrounded by . . . It has to stop.'

But it was he who stopped, as if that were all he had to say. The congregation writhed with embarrassment—then jumped with fright as he suddenly shouted across at the miners, 'What will you do with your dead, now you've left no room to bury them? Where will you look next for a seam of gold? Will you dig up our dead? Will you knock down our houses?' Out of the corner of his eye he saw Valmir Zoderer rise to his feet, and turned to address him—not as an enemy but as an ally. 'You have the words! I've read your poetry in the square! You tell them, Valmir! You have the words to tell them what's happened to this town! They won't listen to me! You tell them what's going to happen next!'

Before Valmir could get over the surprise of being spoken to, Ignatius returned his appeal to the miners. 'I don't condemn your motives! I know you're all hard-working, honest men. I know you only want to provide for your wives and children and parents—an education for your son, a month's rent, medicine for your mother, a piece of clothing to keep yourself covered up. I know how you reason! You think I don't? *Ask Inez da Souza.* Ask her! She knows. She knows that I've picked up a spade myself and dug.'

Inez felt scalded to the very roots of her hair. The blood rushed so loudly through her eardrums that she could barely hear what else he had to say.

'Think what I can do for the poor, with a bag of gold in my fist, I said to myself. Think! I might raise enough for a malaria clinic! Think how much bread I could put into empty bellies. Think how I might even the odds for those helpless, voiceless souls who ran to this town away from landowners who shot them, away from employers who cheated them, away from a world which knows they're fair game to be suckered! I might even afford a lawyer's fees to even up the odds, I thought! *And gold to stop the rot!* Oh Lord, how I wanted that—to pack it in like a dentist packing gold into decaying teeth: to save this town from

crumbling destitution! Listen to how I reasoned it out.

'It can't be bad, I told myself—not the gold itself. Not bad in itself. The Three Wise Men took gold to Bethlehem, didn't they? The Christ child didn't turn it down, did He? "Thanks for the frankincense and myrrh, fellers, but your gold stinks"? There was gold in Eden in the first innocent days of the world. It's there in the Bible. "*And the gold of that land was good.*" That's what I said to myself. I heard myself saying it. I believed it, God knows. Can you tell me I was wrong? Can you say any of that's not true? Any more than I can say to you, "Your wife's better off without a house. Your child's better off without an education."

'You'll go on digging. I know for a fact I'm wasting my breath telling you to stop, because I've felt the same as you're feeling, and I know just how strong that compulsion is to dig. But listen, will you? Listen to what else I can hear at the back of my mind. Listen to what else I *know for a fact*.

'If we go on digging, the destruction will go beyond what you imagine. If we go on digging, everything will get in our way. Doing it for the children's education, are you? Already the children here dig sooner than go to school. Doing it for a fresh chance in life? What kind of future did Amilcar Lopez carve out for himself? Doing it for a bit of security in your old age, are you? Do you think malaria will pass over your tent like the Angel of Death, just because you hang a holy medal on the tent-flap?

'You'll find everything comes between you and the gold: the buildings in this town, the men in the next *barranco*, the Law—even the Dead in their graves. Because once the hunger is there, there's never enough to satisfy it. That's the power of gold. That's the *evil* of gold. It's not the man wanting it . . .' (He stretched out his left hand as far as it would go.) 'It's not the gold itself.' (He reached out with his right fist.) 'It's the danger to everything *standing in between*!'

Valmir, who had been on his feet all this while, took a step forward. Mr da Souza made a restraining grab, but missed him. 'Not now, there's a good chap,' he hissed. 'None of your politics now.' Even Inez, who had begun the day so seething with thoughts of revenge, begged Valmir not to make a speech. But Valmir would not be stopped. Wiping the palms of his hands on his jeans, he stepped up into the choir stalls and turned to face the congregation: he on one side, priest and pulpit on the other.

'*Everything Ignatius has told you is true,*' he shouted, in a voice trembling with emotion—and it was so contrary to anyone's expectations that they stared back at him open-mouthed. 'Also, if you go on digging, the mercury from your separating process will poison the water in the river. The water will poison the fish, the fish will poison anyone who eats them. If you go on digging,' he said, 'the erosion to the substrata combined with the winter rains will cause massive subsidence in . . . I mean, places will start to fall down—cliffs, houses, trees, hills.'

'If you go on living cheek-by-jowl with each other, the malaria is bound to spread,' Ignatius put in.

'Your *donos* will get rich lending you money while you work just to make the repayments on their loans,' said Valmir.

'Your children's best friend will be the drug-dealer.'

'Your only protection will be a loaded shotgun.'

'For the sake of your wife, you'll stay away from her month after month,' said Ignatius.

'And if you go on felling the trees over that way, the topsoil will wash into the river when the rains come, and nothing'll grow there for twenty years!' cried Valmir.

Their voices volleyed from side to side of the church, pinning down the congregation in the crossfire.

'You think you just want a living—nothing more than a living. But believe me! Beyond that there'll be something else. Each time the man next to you gets richer, you feel poorer, don't you? Each time he behaves like a pig, you comfort yourself that there's a man worse than you, even if you do a few things you wouldn't have done in the old days . . .'

'And the cost of living will go on rising—rising, on and on, so you'll have to keep digging, just to keep eating,' said Valmir.

'You want Heaven, and for that you're turning this place into a hell!' said the priest.

'Go on handling mercury and you'll cripple—or blind—or kill yourself!'

Like twin cannon raised up on a defensive position, Valmir and Ignatius blasted away with their own particular ammunition, the priest delivering the spiritual dimension, Valmir inserting the physical, the practical, the particular.

Their volleys struck home, too. They emptied the seats of *garimpeiros*. For in a protest movement started by Eleisar Juca, the local union representative, they stormed out, vowing never to return. 'Where was this town heading before we brought it back alive?' Juca demanded.

'Not to Hell like it is now!' retorted Mr da Souza leaping on to a chair to be seen over the sea of waving arms.

'Papa!' exclaimed Inez, dragging on his braces. 'Don't make an exhibition of yourself!'

'You can't stop progress. The world needs gold,' maintained Juca, at the top of his voice, and the *garimpeiros* stood and cheered him.

'Not at the price of our children!' shrieked a woman in the third row, lobbing a flick-knife into the central aisle. It skidded along the floor, then spun on its hasp like a compass needle seeking True North.

'Those spacemen up there!' cried an aged *garimpeiro* pointing up at the roof with his leather hat. 'Those spacemen need our gold for their space helmets!' His gnarled hands shaped a visor in front of his stone-age face.

'And what do they see through their gold-coated visors?' demanded Valmir, climbing up the outside of Ignatius's pulpit to gain more height. 'The rainforests burning! And fifty million landless Brazilians all trying to climb down a hole in Serra Vazia!' Father Ignatius wiped some of Valmir's spit off one ear, but did not seem greatly put out—

not by the spittle and not by the noisy disarray breaking out in his church. He steadied Valmir with one hand.

Mr da Souza was still balanced on his chair. 'Papa! Papa, get down this instant!' said Inez . . . and while her back was turned, her brother climbed up on a chair too.

'Football!' Maro yelled. 'What we need is football! Who's going to put back our football pitch?!'

Somewhere near the back, Enoque and Honorio Furtado, fêted *desbravadors*, sat with their hats between their knees, looking at the floor. 'But gold's so beautiful,' said Enoque to his brother. 'No one says how beautiful it is.' He did not contribute the comment to the general debate: he did not think his balance was any longer sound enough for climbing on to chairs.

'This place owes its life to gold!' bellowed Eleisar Juca from the door of the church. 'Without the gold mines on the mountain and the gold strike down here, there wouldn't *be* a Vazia town!'

'Well? *Well? Have you seen it lately*?' screamed Mr da Souza, his braces at full stretch.

Eleisar crammed his hat back on to his unblessed head and, like a sheriff at the head of a posse, led the offended *garimpeiros* out through the porch in a state of aggrieved righteousness.

Of course he was denied any grand, sweeping, cinematic exit by the yawning hole in front of the church steps. The posse was obliged to queue in an orderly fashion to mince, arms outstretched like ballerinas, across the nearest available plank.

It was half-way across this plank that Eleisar halted, causing a bottle-neck. By this time, the hostility of the towns-people, roused up by the rhetoric, had brought them herding down the nave to shout afterthoughts at the *garimpeiros*.

Consequently, there was a large audience to witness what happened next. Otherwise—individually—they might never have believed it; might have mistaken it for a trick of the light.

The grey finger of the rubber factory chimney on Lisboa Avenue had protruded above the wooden roofs of Main Street for fifty years. Such a time had passed since the closure of the factory that Maro and Inez had never seen smoke come out of it. It had always stood inert, purposeless. As little children, coming out of church, Maro and Inez had always thought God must have put it there as a fingerpost, pointing the way to Heaven.

Suddenly that grey finger crooked, beckoning, then slid out of sight. The noise arrived from some other direction, having travelled in and out of the houses. A column of dust rose over the spot where the chimney had fallen.

'The factory just fell down!' said Eleisar, balanced on his plank, bounced up and down involuntarily by the jostling of the men behind. 'Damn me but the rubber plant just fell down! That's right behind my house. That might've been my house, that might've!'

Inside the church, Father Ignatius continued to clasp the shoulder of Valmir's shirt, for fear the student fall off the pulpit. Their heads were brought close together. 'Write to the Press,' he said. 'You write letters, don't you? Write to the newspapers and tell them what's happening here. That's where the real power is these days. With the media.'

Valmir nodded, and the cogwheels of his mind began to turn, assembling his words, planning out the first letter. Such thinking restricted his powers of speech. 'I never liked you,' was all he managed to say.

'I never knew you before today,' said Father Ignatius, lowering him carefully to the ground.

'I suppose that's what I meant, really,' said Valmir vaguely, and returned to the storeroom over the shop to write indignant letters of tragic intensity to the newspapers in Rio and Manaus and Brazilia. Writing them was a kind of act of faith in itself since, for those sealed inside Serra Vazia town, it was no longer easy to believe that an outside world existed. Not one that cared.

9

QUEBRADO

(Out of Order)

The rubber factory was gone. Not just its chimney but its whole derelict shell had curtsied down to the ground and slithered into the *barrancos*, filling them with bricks and mortar and pieces of old, rust-red machinery. Fifteen *barrancos* had disappeared, along with several of the men working them. Others, who had been saved by attending Sunday Mass, offered up thanks to Santa Barbara (who fends off lightning strikes, explosions, and pit disasters), salvaged what equipment they could from under the rubble, and looked about for somewhere else to dig.

They were unmoved by Eleisar telling them not to. Realizing the danger to his house, he had been converted instantly to the cause of the townspeople. But in changing sides he had lost his influence. He might have led the miners out of the church, but they had only followed him in the person of El Dorado, King of the *Garimps*. As soon as he opposed the digging, said it must stop because it was undermining the foundations of his house, they drifted away from him—not unfriendly, not disloyal, just intent on their own need for gold.

Every day the danger to his house grew greater. The *garimps* were members of his own union, he said; he ordered them to stop work, but they went on digging. He threatened them with expulsion from the union if they defied him, but they went on digging anyway.

Down the road, the student Valmir Zoderer stood with a shotgun, all day, threatening to blast anyone who laid a spade to the foundations of the drugstore. But Eleisar, who considered himself a cleverer man, appealed to the Law.

He determined to take out a legal injunction to stop the *garimps* digging. So Eleisar flew out on the next *teco-teco* and flew back the next week with the legal document. Everyone saw it. It was very impressive, in the way that only Brazilian legal documents can be, festooned with red wax seals and wound in satin ribbon. He shook it at the *garimps* in the street outside his house. He broke off the costly wax seals in knocking them about the head.

But nothing could undo the fact that, in his absence, the front wall of his house and a section of his roof had collapsed into the street.

All his possessions lay open to prying sunbeams. Small animals had annexed the top of his wardrobe, colonized his chest-of-drawers. And all the floorboards had twanged loose at the skirting board, because the remaining walls were now shifting with every vibration, swaying with every breeze.

The *garimpeiros* shrugged at him, as if to say, 'It was in our way. What else could we do?'

It was at about this time that the *Companhia do Rio Xingu* employed the *despachante* to represent their interest in Serra Vazia. Now, a *despachante* is a very particular breed of man. His function in life is to axe a path for his clients through all obstacles: through the jungles of bureaucracy, the tangled creepers of red tape. In short, he is a Fixer. This one resembled nothing so much as a saki monkey, the long hair on the crown of his head falling forwards in a thick fringe whose ends, poking in his eyes, made him blink incessantly. He had the saki's long beard, too, and woolly coat, though his had been tailored in Lima at the expense of several llamas. Irrespective of the weather he kept it pulled close round him, for inside, in custom-made pockets, he carried a wealth of documents, leaflets, letters, several wallets with just a little money in each (in case he was robbed) and, reputedly, several passports of different nationalities. The *despachante*, it seemed, inhabited as many countries as the Amazon river.

The *Companhia* employed him to go from door to door of every house in Main Street and Lisboa Avenue, offering to buy the buildings on their behalf. If the town could be cleared—razed to the ground, then they could bring in big machinery to extract whatever there was worth having beneath the wooden houses.

'Sell it, why don't you? Before it falls down,' the Fixer would say, pointing out signs of subsidence, the alarming gaps around the window, the bowing planks, the sagging rooflines. Then he would offer them for their home the price of a second-hand bike. It was a buyer's market, after all. 'Good of me to offer you anything at all,' he said. 'The place'll fall down tomorrow, like as not.'

'Get out of my home or I'll shoot you where you stand!' said Valmir Zoderer, prodding the barrel of his gun about in the deep vegetation of the Fixer's beard.

In the background Mr and Mrs da Souza sat staring at one another across a single shared tin of tapioca pudding, their spoons motionless with horror in mid-air. Their son and daughter stood shoulder-to-shoulder behind Valmir, their fingers in the belt loops of his jeans, nodding their heads and murmuring. 'That's right. You go.'

'You push off and tell them what they can do with their money.'

'Nobody's going to dig under *our* home.'

'Nobody's going to knock down *this* house.'

After the Fixer had gone, Valmir sank into a chair. The gun between his knees shook. Maro and Inez looked at one another and quite suddenly, after months of enmity, hugged each other close. Just for a moment, the feeling of one-ness was so powerful that it seemed something good had just happened and nothing bad at all.

'We have to do something,' said Inez, bending her face over the top of his hair to whisper in her brother's ear.

'Drive them all away.'

'Before it's too late.'

'Before we lose everything.' They nodded earnestly, to encourage one another.

Mrs da Souza sucked her spoon clean then pushed back her chair. The back legs lodged in a sag in the carpet and she almost overbalanced: a hole had already opened up between the floorboards. 'Valmir's letters will save us,' she said, frightened by her children's innocent, ignorant fearlessness. 'All we have to do is to let the world outside hear what's happening here. All we have to do is shame the *Companhia* and the *garimps* into going away.' But whatever she said out loud, plainly neither Mrs da Souza nor her husband were convinced. Could everything be put to rights just by the power of the Press?

'Maybe we should consider the offer that the *Companhia* . . .' said Mr da Souza, but the room turned on him such a unanimous look of horror that he never spoke the words out loud. And so his chance to sell up and leave Serra Vazia once and for all, with a few dollars in his pocket and his family safe and sound, came and went, without hope of return. He felt it go. He felt despair fall on him like an undermined house. It felt just like the lights going out.

Like it? The lights *had* just gone out! The whole room was plunged into darkness. With a painful straining, their eyes adjusted to the pale cast of moon lightening the windows. There was a noise of sash windows opening, of men shouting curses. A power cut had blacked out the whole town. An industrious *garimpeiro,* working by the splendour of Vazia town's new streetlights, had severed the power lines.

Next day, the liquidizers in Orlando's Juice Bar were *quebrado*—out of order. In Disco Tony the amplifiers were silent, the mirror ball still, the disco-complex struck dumb. The giant colour television in the square hung from its pole, the screen and tube dislocated from the casing like a great grey eyeball dislodged from its socket, blinded. With the power gone, there was nothing to stop an enterprising *garimpeiro* from starting work on the town square, prising up its paving stones, gouging out its hard core. A kind of metalwork beaver's dam of spindly tubular chairs was swept together outside the *churrascaria*.

The candles in the Church of Santa Barbara no longer flickered their orange filaments in supplication to the Almighty.

All of a sudden, Vazia took a step backwards in time. With the electricity gone, lightbulbs hung from their cables like cankered fruit sucked empty by wasps. At first, people moved about after dark with oil lanterns and candles, but finding they had too little light to cross safely the dark yawning canyon of the street, they scurried to bed—went to ground like rabbits, to await the comforting light of dawn. Anything could happen in such a darkness.

The Amazon jungle pressed closer, breathed more hotly, bristled its leafy fur, like a wild beast held at bay only by the last glimmerings of a campfire. The stars plunged closer, with no upward swords of light to fend them off. The cacophonous silence of jungle night, always before dented a little by the hammering of music or the clamour of the TV, pressed in now like the spiked walls of some horrific torture chamber. Somehow the tinny squeaks of car radios and transistors were overwhelmed and smothered by the suffocating noise of blackness. Spider monkeys shrieked, invisible on the housetops. Snakes colonized the *barrancos*. Giant inias moved down river unseen, but their webbed feet could be heard as loud as oars, driving them through the current.

The *cantina*, of course, stood throbbing in its own pool of self-generated brilliance, burning valuable petrol in an arrogant flourish of light. Throughout the night, shadowy figures braved the pitfalls of the darkened streets to buy some plain package at the bright doorway of the camper-van. But for the most part, it was not safe to go out at night. Men are prepared to commit worse crimes under cover of darkness, and the deeper the darkness, the deeper Man's wickedness.

'I can't be your friend any more, Enoque,' said Maro.

The *garimpeiro* cradled his pet woolly monkey like a teddy bear. He seemed about to suck his thumb, but was in fact only raising a hand to cover one eye. 'I'm sorry to hear that, da Souzzz. Why's that, then?'

'Because you're a miner and the miners are busting up the town. Knocking the houses down. Killing people.'

'I never killed nobody,' said Enoque, wounded.

'No, I didn't mean . . . I never said you did but . . . well. We keep telling the *garimps* to go away and you don't go. You just go on digging and digging and digging . . .'

'We wou'n't never go under your place, if that's what you're edgy about. We won't. Honest. Not like they did to Juca's place.'

'Not you, maybe, but someone . . .' Maro felt as if he had just refused Enoque a place on his football team. The look of uncomprehending hurt on the gnarled face reproached him with unjust cruelty.

'We got to dig, see. We got to dig where the gold is. We're *garimps*, see? Honorio and I. That's what we does.' It was as if he had answered some calling too holy to be ignored, as if he had been conscripted by Fate to serve in the great army of *garimpeiros*, reshaping the face of Brazil with fork and spade and hose. The tayra sitting on Enoque's hat bared its teeth at Maro, but Enoque did not. He simply snorted through his blocked sinuses, swatted inaccurately at a fly on Maro's chest, and soothed his woolly monkey with hands that continuously shook. 'Your Dadda tell you to cut loose of me?' he asked, wistfully resigned. 'He jacked in working for us yesterday.'

Maro could not resist the lie, the temptation to blame someone other than himself for ending the friendship. 'Yes, that's it. Dad says I mustn't hang around with you no more. Now the digging's gone crazy-mad.'

This cheered Enoque a little. His features seemed to be undergoing a re-organization, like Mrs da Souza's furniture sometimes did. 'Well, you got to do what your Dadda says. No oddsing that. None. But I'll be sorry not to drink an *açai* with you of a morning, son, and that's no lie.' He took his hat off and shook hands with Maro, making a formal deep bow. The lie weighed all the heavier in Maro's hand, as if the handshake had pressed lead deep into his palm. 'Good to know you, Master da Souzzz . . . Please give my regards to your pretty sister.'

'Good to know you, Mr Furtado, sir. Please give my regards to your brother.'

At the Hotel d'Ouro, despite the blackout, the proprietor made a last-ditch stand against the Legions of Darkness. Buying up every candle and lantern the *cantina* could supply, he even risked angering the *cantineiro* by shopping at Vazia Drugstore and buying all Mr da Souza's supplies of candles and nightlights too. So that back at the hotel he held court, shining like Lucifer in the depths of the Dark Regions. The windows blazed. The insect screens swarmed—one dense mass of moths, bugs and flies dancing to the music of Senhora Ferretti's rumbas. There were so many wicks burning that the Dealer could read the stockmarket prices from his newspaper. There was so much artificial light that the representative of *Companhia do Rio Xingu* could type up contracts of house-purchase on his lap-top, battery-powered computer. In fact there were so few shadows that the Fixer could find nowhere but the darkness of his room to conduct business with his shadier clientele.

In her candlelit grotto, the monumental Senhora Ferretti sweated in the great heat of burning wax, though her weary features lost ten or fifteen years in the flattering light, and her eyes shone as though they were full of tears.

Meanwhile, by the light of one Advent candle, and wrapped in a stony darkness deeper than night, a band of conspirators met. Maro and Inez, Valmir and Father Ignatius sat in the crypt of Santa Barbara Church. They had no plot to hatch as yet—though like broody, squatting chickens, they felt the longing to hatch *something*. They had only the dark discontent of conspirators binding them together. Ostensibly they were keeping watch: a civil guard intent on protecting the town's church from overnight digging.

'One of us ought to be watching the graveyard,' said Valmir.

'One of us ought to be watching the shop,' said Inez.

But alone out there they could have done nothing. Together they felt the strength of solidarity. And so, for an hour each night they talked about how terrible the situation was, how right they had been all along.

Startled to be invited, Inez and Maro sat silent at first, waiting to be treated as children. But crisis, it seemed, had promoted them to an honorary adulthood. It was exciting to be consulted, to be allowed an opinion. Inez was not sure how or whether her feelings towards Ignatius had been altered by everything that had happened. She only knew that it had been a lonely, desolate time while she hated and despised him. She was only too relieved to put the hatred behind her and forgive Ignatius his moment of weakness. There was something adult-feeling about that, too: forgiving a grown man.

When the topics of greed and wickedness palled, they talked about music and football, and told stories and jokes, then saw each other home by the fat light bursting the seams of the gross Hotel d'Ouro. The two children felt like adults and the two adults felt young again—or at least renewed enough to hold out against the forces of evil a while longer.

At first light, Maro was woken by the sound of an aeroplane, a *teco-teco* passing overhead. He lay half asleep, half awake, letting the thoughts trickle through his head like light through gaping wood shingles. He would have liked to go on seeing Enoque, but could not. Enoque and Honorio were the Enemy—just two of the unstoppable *garimpeiros* demolishing his world. Termites attack an anthill at its base, and if the soldier ants don't swarm to its defence, soon the red corridors, the ochre turrets and stairways, the dusty chambers white with babies or golden with queens, are poisoned with formic acid and falling, falling, falling.

Why defend it? Was the Drugstore so much of a royal palace? Hardly.

A string tied to his bedhead ran out of his window and in at Valmir's—an alarm system to alert the man with the empty shotgun if the store came under attack—to tell him to man the parapets. But was it such a marvellous castle as to merit defending?

It was just home. That was all Maro could give himself by way of an answer. It was home. Though no early morning smell of dough or hot bread rose through the floorboards these days; though this was not the ideal place for a football star to be born; though the store had always intruded on his life (there were shelves of baked beans over his hammock where other boys had Subbuteo); still it was home. He belonged here—belonged not *to* anyone— simply belonged. Though he had never looked before with any fondness at the knotholes in the walls, the cobwebs and rime of silvery dust, he could see their charm now. This house represented the roots from which he had grown, the springboard from which he would leap into the world, the nest from which he had still to take flight.

Now it was being undermined; men wanted to undermine it, heartened by the thought that when it fell down round them, they could reach the gold under his dining-room floor, the gold under his dining-room table, the gold under his Sunday lunch. *'Well, they won't!'* said Maro aloud.

And Inez, who had been lying awake thinking the selfsame thoughts, turned over, her eyes wide and defiant: 'No, they won't, will they?'

10

PRESS GANG

By the middle of October, the Hotel d'Ouro had all its bedrooms occupied, and guests sleeping on couches in the lobby too. For the plane Maro had heard, and the seventeen after that, had brought the Press to town.

Like birds colonizing a tree, they roosted in the Hotel, journalists not just from Marabá and Manaus and Rio de Janeiro, but the local correspondents for overseas papers— the *New York Times, Le Monde,* the *Daily Telegraph, Die Welt*: an aviary so varied that it brought the locals out-of-doors to birdwatch for the yellow flash of a camera, the feathery flourish of a pen.

Valmir, rushing his breakfast of tinned baking apples, snatched up his folder of notes and rolled up his socks over his best jeans to protect them from mud splashes. 'I thought I'd show them the river while I go into the environmental aspects,' he said, 'then take them up on the church roof for an overview of the town. Ignatius has given me the keys.'

'Can I come?' said Maro, and Valmir was so cheerful that he did not object. On the way to the hotel he even confided in Maro his secret ambitions. He hoped today to impress the journalists so much with his grasp of the facts and his professionalism that one or other would make him the offer of a job. Perhaps after they went home, he could act as their 'man on the spot', recounting in pithy articles the town's last-minute salvation from the brink of disaster. His similes would catch the attention of a chief sub-editor, his plangent pleas would touch the hearts of readers. His colourful descriptions would fire their imaginations. Other work would come of it: features perhaps on ecology, conservation, justice for the Indians . . . In the time it took for the stewed apple to give him stomach ache, he had mapped out his entire future. Those men stirring in the luxury of Hotel d'Ouro bedrooms, leaping from their beds even now and showering, with pencils clenched between their teeth, were the heroes of Valmir's world: the communicators, the men with the power to spill the Truth in the world's lap like a morning fresh egg.

He and Maro had sat in the bar of the hotel for an hour before the first of the journalists appeared. When he did, he was fiddling with a mobile telephone held up against his head, whose wagging aerial, like a huge antenna, made him look like a longicorn beetle. He hitched one leg over a bar stool and told Valmir to get him a whisky.

'They don't serve alcohol here, sir,' said Valmir. 'Because of the state mines down the road, you see.'

'Don't give me problems, give me a whisky. Whisky and water, half-and-half.'

'Permit me to introduce myself,' said Valmir walking down the bar with his hand outstretched. 'I was the man who wrote filling you in about this business.'

'Hey, Wal. Come and help. I can't get a whisky out of this aboriginal.'

A second journalist stumbled down the last of the stairs looking as though he had slept the night in the *barrancos*. He swore at the staircase and he swore at the lock on the bar. He wriggled under the flap and rooted about amid a noise of tinkling bottles, emerging with a bottle of whisky and a glass of *chope* beer he had already poured himself. Holding the cloudy beer up to the light to watch the little shreds of growing bacteria swirl about, he swore at the beer as well. Then he went through to the lobby where he stood in the open doorway. 'What a hole,' he said to the early morning sunshine.

Valmir, at his shoulder said, 'Yes. Currently it's two-hundred metres long, ten metres wide just here and approaching fifteen metres deep.'

The journalist looked at him as if *he* were the longicorn beetle. Valmir turned back to find the whole bar filling up with dishevelled, discontented gentlemen of the Press. The hotel manager opened the bar himself to cater for their thirst. And there they stayed.

The aviary was full. The giant toucan with bands of shaving cream across his nose, helped himself to fruit from an ornamental basket before cramming his beak and pockets with the rest. A carrion crow tugged at a rare steak, using tomato sauce to cool it. A blue-headed parrot, his jowls living with dark bristles, discussed the European Cup with a harpy-eagle of slow and ponderous flight. When Valmir moved between them, offering to guide them through the history and geography of the catastrophe, they looked up out of hooded, bloodshot eyes, then went back to their conversation.

Valmir climbed half-way up the staircase. 'Are you coming, then?' he asked, in a loud voice. Maro was the only one who jumped to his feet with enthusiasm.

'Yes! Just come and see what they've done to our football pitch!'

'We'll wait for you on the front steps,' said Valmir. 'Rubber shoes are essential. I've arranged a photo-opportunity for later on.'

An hour later, only Inez had joined them on the front steps. 'Perhaps you shouldn't have mentioned the rubber shoes,' said Maro. 'They didn't look the types to have rubber shoes.' But though the sun continued to shine, the journalists continued to huddle together in the hotel bar, as if against the cold.

'Maybe they're afraid to go out alone. In case they get shot,' said Inez 'Maybe they want to stick together.'

Valmir nodded. Sometimes, out there in the jungle, thirty different species of bird would gang together to hunt down a communal meal of flies. On the other hand, the puff bird sits still all day on a branch, waiting for insects to fly into its open mouth.

From indoors the sound of laughter grew louder than the chug-chugging of a nearby generator. Looking along the front of the building, Valmir saw the faces of his heroes peer out through the speckled filth of the sealed windows, then turn away with a laughing, disbelieving shake of the head.

They only stayed in Serra Vazia for as long as it took the *teco-tecos* to return, though some treated themselves to a beach holiday on the Nordeste coast because their desk editors had allowed them a week to cover the story. They duly filed those stories, of course, and sold other versions to the news agencies. The tabloids had just the right slot for them, on pages entitled *Fancy That!* or *Would You Believe It!?* and *Stranger than Fiction*. The quality papers placed the articles in those bottom-left-hand corners where readers knew to look for an amusing anecdote. Something to cheer them up amid the grimmer world news.

Some were witty. Most adopted a more comic-book, slapstick style. '*It's going-going-gone! as greedy garimps go for gold!*' The hilarious irony of Eleiser Juca's story had particularly appealed to them: '"*I was undermined!*" *says union boss*' ... '*Union man raises roof as floor falls in*' ... '*And the walls came tumbling down!*'

'Look at it this way,' said Father Ignatius to his bewildered congregation, tearing a copy of the *New York Times* into shreds and showering the pieces down over the side of his pulpit. 'If what's happening here is a matter for laughter, think how much worse off people must be in the world out there, whose tragedies do move even journalists to pity.'

Because of the power failure, a supply of real candles had replaced the consol of electric imitation ones. Several had been lit, too. Then the box had been stolen, but the thief had stopped short of blowing out those already lit. So a few whorls and stalagmites had formed on the church floor, beneath the dripping candles. The Baby collected them up, squeezing the soft, warm wax into satisfying pats. The flames were more intriguing, more collectable still, but out of reach.

So when, after dark that night, the same dancing orange could be seen escaping the Hotel d'Ouro, The Baby set off, determined to collect some of the delectable lozenges of light: an entomologist in search of fireflies. The lack of candles at the store meant that, for half an hour, nobody noticed The Baby was missing.

The swaying beat of the samba was an additional lure. Senhora Ferretti was taking requests from her audience, standing at a piano to vamp out her own accompaniment. The wires of the piano were starting to sense the coming of the rainy season—losing their voice like vocal chords succumbing to laryngitis. But La Senhora's voice was as powerful as ever, belting out the wild, intoxicating lyrics that had comforted the poor in their slums for generations. Now she was singing them to the less-than-poor: the Dealer, the Fixer, the *donos*, the *do Rio Xingu* rep, to gun sellers and a couple of *bamburrados* . . .

> '*Hummingbird sips from the lily tree*
> *Fishing-bird dips in the chilly sea*
> *Honeycomb drips for the honey bee.*
> *I ain't gonna cry no more.*'

When the piano began to move, it was only very slowly—over the hem of her dress, crushing the sequins like brittle bugs. She moved with it, her eyes compensating for the shift of keys beneath her fingertips. Then, as the piano gathered momentum, she moved round in front of it and blocked its progress. It thumped her in the back, but her great bulk was enough to stop it rolling off the edge of the stage on to the police inspector. The first the audience knew of the grotto's unease was when a potted palm crossed the stage in a leafy glissando and embraced the microphone stand.

The myriad candles wedged into winebottles shivered and shook, then recovered with a communal gout of black smoke. Smuts floated through the air looking for a shoulder to settle on. 'Would you shift please, sir?' said La Senhora politely to the police inspector. 'We seem to be on the move here.' And he had no sooner snatched up his wine bottle and glass than the piano circumnavigated the singer and rolled backwards off the stage.

The grotto constricted like a mouth coughing, and all its contents rushed outwards, scattering the band and terrifying the hostesses. Senhora Ferretti alone clung to the backdrop, reefing in two armfuls of slippery cloth as the stage raked further and further under her. It was she who felt the first draught of cold air sucked in around the back wall by the burning candles, as the Hotel d'Ouro attempted to fill its congested lungs. It seemed as if the hotel was subsiding face-first into Main Street, but it was not. The stage collapsed because the rear wall of the hotel had suddenly pulled free of the roof. It rained down now as separate planks, faster and faster into the vast hole in Obidos Street.

Singly the planks seemed too flimsy to do harm. The owner of the *cantina* watched them break loose and flutter down like oak seeds, hardly expecting them to do damage. And yet their size only looked small in comparison with the great mass of the hotel, and when falling planks of wood five metres long began to stove in his roof, his windows, the metal bodywork, and chrome roof rack, he pulled his wife under the bed and howled. Next time he dared to look out, the back of the Hotel d'Ouro was made merely of cloth billowing outwards ahead of a tidal wave of light. A round, short-legged woman hung from a panel of cloth trying to keep herself from going overboard into the sea of darkness and mud that gaped beneath her feet. Like a liner, the Hotel d'Ouro was slowly sliding stern-under, foundering.

With the sudden inrush of night air, the ranks and banks of candles sprang up again. But the vibration of the floor slithering over the mud and stones on which it was laid shook the candle stubs out of their various holders, and they too became loose cargo rolling about amid the dropped cigars, the drink tumblers, the table knives, and metal trays. The crap dice bounded eagerly, misguidedly in among a spilled bowl of sugar cubes. A slot-machine suddenly played a frenzied fanfare and vomited up a jackpot of coins.

Paper napkins conspired with the candles to flare upwards and ignite the hems of tablecloths. The room began to fade, like a bad television picture, a greyish haze smearing out all detail, and a noxious smell growing. The plastic palm trees burned with a pluming roar, their long leaves curling downwards to drop molten fire on to the green baize and polished wood and nylon carpet. A thick black reek stuffed up the room, a smoke as thick and tangible as black wool. Outside in the street, the *cantineiro* could feel the heat leaning against his van, hear it expanding the chrome of his bumper, breaking the surviving lightbulbs with a ping-ping-ping. He remembered the tenders full of diesel oil and petrol, and came out from under the bed, and stood his little wife in the sink, shouldering her out through the small fanlight window because the door was locked against robbers and he could not find the key. She stood on the bonnet for a few moments, whooping coughs and fright as the shattering windows of Hotel d'Ouro spangled down on her in a glittering rain. Then she jumped into the deep, cold, dark *barranco* alongside, without being able to see its bottom. Blundering along, like a First World War soldier under fire in the trenches, she sobbed her husband's name over and over again without daring to look back. Then she collided with something soft and scaly and live.

With the soft thump of mortars firing, the fuel tenders and petrol tank of the *cantina* exploded—one, two, three. Plumes of fire as tall as the rubber factory chimney had once been, rose in monstrous imitation of candle flames, and the whole of Obidos Street was lit, bright as day. The *cantineiro's* wife found she had collided with the rump of Senhora Ferretti.

All along the rooftops, an audience of monkeys was captured in the orange glare, shocked into a stillness. There were owl monkeys curled up in the new forked TV aerials, howler monkeys with mouths agape, woolly monkeys like children's teddies propped along a cot rail. From their seat in the upper circle, the monkeys watched the little drama unfold below them. Like an audience, unmoved. Or like gods looking down from Heaven.

A simple outbreak of fire would have trapped the hotel's occupants by the dozen. But because the d'Ouro had caught light in the very act of subsidence, it disintegrated around them, plank by plank, then carried its skeleton of fire away over their terrified heads and sprawled headlong into the pit of Main Street, pitching up against the house opposite which also burned to the ground.

The *cantineiro* did squeeze through his fanlight in time to escape. The Dealer, still holding a palm-heart *empada*, the Fixer still holding a hostess round the waist, the Company Man still cradling his lap-top computer, the croupier still clutching one silver sandal, all met up with him, his wife and the fat samba singer in the muddy trench behind where the hotel had stood. There La Senhora led them in the singing of baleful hymns till morning restored their spirits sufficiently to put God and La Senhora behind them.

A pity that the Press had not stayed another week. The fire would have given them something really exciting to write about. A pity, yes. For if they had had to run from the Hotel d'Ouro with their clothes alight and had lost all their possessions to the flames, it might just have increased their sensitivity to the pain of other people's comical little tragedies.

11

CONSPIRATORS

The search was frenzied. Waiters in smudged white jackets threw tables aside and scrabbled among heaps of broken crockery. *Garimps* burned themselves on tubular chairs still hot and smoking, and cut themselves on the shards of wine bottles in their haste. The Dealer, above the ping of contracting metal and avalanches of ash, bellowed out of smoke-filled lungs: 'Look! Look! Look, will you? A hundred cruzeiros to the man who finds it!' He heaved doors aside, kicked out at melted lengths of plumbing and tangles of wiring. Meanwhile, the manager of the hotel ran up and down the roof of an adjacent building, directing anyone and everyone: 'Look under there! Lift that up! No, not there, you fool! Shift that bath!'

On the edge of the smouldering ruins stood Mrs da Souza, her stillness exaggerated by the manic activity of those scrambling over the charred remains. Her feet were sunk in the mud so that she looked like one of her own black orchids, blasted and overblown. Her hands were in her hair. Her baby was lost among all this devastation. Though her husband spoke to her from alongside, she did not seem to hear him. The look on her face said that she thought herself dead and in Hell, and to tell the truth, the scene of the fire closely resembled some medieval pictures of Hell: the smoke, the heat, the jumping, scrabbling bodies, the desperate search for something lost.

'Here it is! I've found it!'

Mrs da Souza's eyes flickered in the direction of the shout, but without expectation. She could see her son and daughter balancing on the burned out promontary of the staircase but could not summon the voice to tell them to be careful.

'That's a toilet cistern, you idiot!' shrieked the hotel manager from the roof. 'Can't you see the chain?'

They were looking not for The Baby, of course, but for the hotel safe-deposit box crammed with the gold and cash and bonds, contracts, receipts, wages, and promisory notes of a month's gold dealing. The fortune and ruin of the hotel's staff, management and all its occupants depended on finding it. If the Dealer was wiped out financially, several *garimpeiros* would go down with him, penniless, all their work gone for nothing.

Only the da Souza family and their neighbours were looking for The Baby, also lost on the night of the fire.

'Here! You! Help me lift this!' panted the Dealer staggering in a slurry of mud, trying to find the purchase to move the hotel piano. The fire had reduced it to a chassis like the hulk of a metal ship rigged with piano wire. His efforts roused jangling, jolly music, but failed to lift the cast-iron frame. Four *garimps* and the barman leapt down among the amputated piano legs and pulled away the last shreds of charred wood, the exertion making them grunt and swear. Even when they saw what was underneath they had to leave go and let the piano drop back down: the weight was too much for them. 'It's there! Did you see it? It's under there!' The Dealer yelled the good news up at the roof, recognizing that the hotel manager had most to lose after him.

'Has it held together?'

'Won't know till we get it open!'

'Somebody bring a crowbar!'

'Where are the keys?'

'Someone bring me a gun. There's fifty-thousand in that box!'

'Where's that crowbar, for God's sake!'

'There's a baby over here.'

'Never mind no crummy baby. Bring me a crowbar!'

'A baby, see? And fifty million candle stubs. It's cornered the market in candle stubs, look at it.'

'A crowbar, for the love of God!'

There was much mention more of God's love that morning, but not by the Dealer. He and the manager found, to their immeasurable relief, that the contents of the safe-deposit box were unharmed by the firestorm. The Fixer went on moping, for he had lost his precious coat in the confusion, and as he said, not less than eighty-seven times, his whole life was wrapped up in that coat. But the Dealer had suffered no such loss. A new room was found for him—an impromptu office, located over the *Banco do Brasil*, loaned by a sycophantic bank manager. And considering he still had his bodyguards to fetch him palmheart *empadas*, the whole arrangement suited him rather better than before. He had always found the operatic samba music rising through the hotel floorboards an irritating distraction.

So it was with a puff of exasperation that the Dealer heard the familiar tones of La Senhora Ferretti from the street outside. His transistor radio was a whorl of melted plastic, welded to the wreckage, somewhere down there. But not the singer. She seemed disagreeably indestructible, rampaging up and down the roof of her flat, singing 'Celeste Aida' at the top of her voice and calling out to passers by—'The da Souzas' baby's been found, you know! Safe and well! . . . Yes . . . isn't it! A miracle! A miracle! Thank God! Thank God! Thank God!'

'We have to do something,' said the conspirators in the crypt. Their number had grown recently, of course, as more and more of the gold-strike's victims took shelter there and sought out the companionship of their neighbours. Their town and their world were tumbling around them. There was Mundicarmo and her mother, still dressed in black mourning for Amilcar. There was Eleiser Juca, homeless but for a bed in Ignatius's house. There was Tony from his darkened and silent disco, Orlando fresh from his dry liquidizers and cracked mirrors. And there was Senhora Ferretti, rocking the da Souza baby on her lap.

'We have to form an army and drive them out of town,' someone said.

'I couldn't condone any violence,' said Father Ignatius. 'Not against people anyway.'

'As I see it, we have two separate problems here: the Indians and the *garimps*,' said Senhora Ferretti.

In the corner of the crypt, Inez sat with her knees drawn up against her chest, resentful to the point of speechlessness. She refused to say a word in the presence of That Woman. She could not believe the ease with which the Ferretti traitor had won back her Acceptability in the eyes of the others—people she had betrayed with her singing and her piano playing and her shiny black dress. It was one thing to forgive Father Ignatius his bout of gold fever. He had been tempted by all the right kind of things—by the wish to do good with the wealth he might dig up. But Senhora Ferretti! She had made an exhibition of herself, singing and playing for the very people who were tearing the town apart, saving her cruzeiros for the day she could get out of Vazia, abandon her home town and never come back. She had made spivs and villains and black marketeers sentimentally happy with her songs. She had set *garimpeiros* whistling. She had taken wages from the hands of that fat cat hotel manager. She was a *collaborator*. Did she think she could change camps at this late hour? Just because her palmy grotto had burned down? Just because her piano was reduced to cheese-wire and ash? Did she think she could sue for re-entry to the ranks of respectable Christians and be let back in?

Apparently she did. Apparently she was right. For here she sat, an intruder on the secret society of friends who met in the crypt, trying to behave as if nothing had ever happened, masquerading as the old blue-frocked village schoolteacher.

Inez looked about her for allies. Valmir clearly agreed with her: he had not said a word all evening. Come to think of it, he had not said a word for a week.

'Even if we could muster the whole town,' Senhora Ferretti was saying, 'I'm afraid we would be the losers in a straightforward confrontation.'

'I agree with La Senhora,' said Father Ignatius (even though Inez fixed him with a look of mortification). 'This isn't *A Fistful of Dollars*. We're not facing up to a band of villains with black hats on their heads and murder in their hearts. We're up against a thousand desperate folk a bit like us, with a thousand different reasons for digging, and too many griefs to care what grief they give to others.'

'Yes, I wouldn't like anyone to shoot Enoque Furtado,' Maro piped up.

'Well, we know just how much the power of the Law helped Eleiser,' La Senhora went on and (incredibly!) everyone nodded and murmured their assent and listened attentively. 'We've seen the best the Authorities can do, and local government. And we've seen the Power of the Press, ha!'

Valmir flushed scarlet, his protruding ears burned purple at the rims. His eyes appeared to fill with tears. He pressed his lips together and they swelled with pent up emotion. Then he hid his face behind his knees, as Inez herself was doing.

' . . . So it seems to me, we can either evacuate now— pack up whatever belongings we can carry and get out before the roofs come down round our ears . . .' (She waited for her audience to stiffen in outraged defiance.) ' . . . or we can *give the gold diggers a good reason to leave*.' She had certainly lost none of her classroom skills; she riveted their attention. 'And what do you think it would take, Inez da Souza, for the gold-diggers and the dealers and the fixers and the gun-runners to get up and go?' Her eyes fell on Inez as they had fallen since, as a terrified six-year-old, she first sat down at a desk in Serra Vazia School.

'Another gold-strike, Senhora,' said Inez. 'Somewhere else.' She said it because she found the words in her mouth. She did not know where the idea came from: it was as if La Senhora had planted it there. 'Another gold-strike. Somewhere else.'

'Exactly!' If she had had her red pencil in her hand, Senhora Ferretti would undoubtedly have made a tick on the floor of the crypt. 'It was rumour that brought them all here. We'll use rumour to move them all on. If the stick won't work, maybe a carrot will shift the donkey.'

Suddenly everyone was talking at once.

'Where? Where?'

'Somewhere uninhabited. Not like this.'

'Somewhere foul!'

'If they hear it on the Radio Peão . . .'

'How? How do we do it?'

'They'll never believe one of us.'

'It's got to come from outside.'

'In the newspapers!'

'How do we get it started?'

'Do any of us have kin in Marabá?'

'It'll work! It will work! It will!'

'Hush. Please. My friends, please.' Though Father Ignatius stood up, his raised hands could not restrain the commotion in the crypt as La Senhora's simple solution to all their problems resurrected their spirits. Mr and Mrs da Souza embraced, Maro and Inez wrestled on the floor. Mundicarmo and her mother lifted their black mantillas to kiss. Tony slapped all four walls to accompany himself in singing *The Deadwood Stage*:

' . . . Wo! whip crack away! whip crack away! whip crack away!'

Even Eleiser Juca, who had no home left to save, showed a certain vengeful pleasure in the thought of putting one over on the men who had undermined his house. La Senhora and The Baby smiled serenely at one another, nose-to-nose.

110

'It wasn't the fire,' she said softly to the child, and it was as if no one else was intended to hear, though Inez felt compelled to eavesdrop. 'It wasn't really the fire's doing, though I suppose one always sees things more plainly in the close proximity of Death. Priorities. The things that matter most. When I heard you were lost, I thought, let them knock down my house, then. Let them swallow up the hotel and the shops and common decency and Law and Order and good manners and cleanliness. Let them eat up the whole ugly town: I never liked it. *But don't let them take that baby.* That they have no right to do. That no one has a right to do. That's not a cost worth paying. For that I would bury them in their own *barrancos* under fifteen metres of mud.' And she looked sideways at Inez, and Inez saw that it had all been said to her and not to The Baby at all.

While around him the Conspirators of Vazia celebrated their renewed hope, Valmir Zoderer stayed crouched under his pall of gloom, his face as long as a five act play, lost in thought. Father Ignatius tried to make him feel better by assigning to him the first blow of the campaign. 'Hush! Quietly now. Secrecy is everything. Listen. Valmir Zoderer here must send in bogus articles to all the newspapers. What editor's going to query a story about a gold-strike, even if he doesn't know who submitted it? Up in the Nordeste, somewhere, maybe. Where there's hardly a soul about and no trees to uproot . . .'

'I'll never write another word,' said Valmir portentously. There was a general intake of breath.

Father Ignatius crouched down to look into his face. 'What's the matter, Valmir?'

Valmir appeared to wash his face with the palms of both hands. It did not remove the anguish. 'I wrote to the Government and they sent in the army—sewed up the election then abandoned us. I wrote to the papers to come, and see what happened? Look what I managed.'

From every pocket in his jacket, shirt and jeans, and from every section of his wallet, he drew out newspaper cuttings and spread them on the floor. He had clearly read them often, for they were dog-eared and perforated at the folds. The light was too poor to read by, but the people in the crypt still recoiled a little. They knew the contents and were instantly depressed by them.

'I made the town a laughing stock, didn't I. I gave thousands of readers a comic story to snigger over at breakfast. "Hey! Listen to this. There's some place up the Amazon where they've dug so deep for gold that all the houses have fallen in the hole! Tee-hee-hee! Isn't that the funniest thing you ever heard? All that gold and—whoops—nowhere to put it. What spadeheads there are in the world! Greedy beggars. Serves 'em right. The *caboclos* dug a hole and the town fell into it! Ho! Ho! Ho!"' Eleisar leaned across and, snatching the cutting out of Valmir's hand, screwed it into a ball. 'You see? That's what my letter-writing did for this town last time. I made it a laughing stock. A joke.'

'The Press did that, not you,' protested Ignatius, but Valmir had shut his mouth, as if words were now to him as meat to a vegetarian, eschewed for ever.

'Then do it in person, Zoderer, and get your own back on them,' said Senhora Ferretti in the slow, wicked, mirthful tones of temptation. Her eyes blazed with gleeful menace. 'Go to Marabá with Ignatius here and play the *bamburrado*. Make as if you've struck it really rich. Get your own back on those pressmen and save the town while you're about it. Give them one in the eye, Zoderer. Do it for Vazia. Do it for your friends here. But do it!'

So, like the first ice-breaker of spring cleaving the frozen sea, the redoubtable Senhora set the plot in motion once again and hauled Valmir up out of the pit of self-hatred. 'By God, I'll do it!' he exclaimed. 'I'll go. I'll pretend to be a *garimpeiro* who's struck the ultimate vein. The biggest strike since '74! We'll have all Marabá buzzing inside the week!'

The conspirators began to laugh. Their laughter came back at them off the walls much louder, as though the dead interred beneath the floor of the beleaguered church were also rejoicing in the plot. So they did not hear—the Living or the Dead—the bang of the church door overhead or the tread of mud-cushioned feet.

'Bless us, Father,' said Mrs da Souza snatching hold of Ignatius's hand and thrusting it into the air. 'Bless our plan. Ask God's help to make it work! Won't you? Please!'

Father Ignatius's fingers folded themselves for benediction, then his eye caught Valmir's and he paused—hesitated to place an atheist under obligation to a God he did not believe in.

'*Would* God bless a lie?' asked Valmir, full of philosophical curiosity.

'With so much else to occupy Him, I'd've thought He'd appreciate people showing a little initiative,' Mrs da Souza chipped in in her brusque, businesslike way. 'We can ask, at least.'

Valmir looked up at the priest's pale fingers raised towards the massy, impenetrable stone ceiling of the crypt. And above that hung the nasty tin roof and above that the poisoned stratosphere, the littered ionosphere, and unbreathable spaces of the cosmos. Then he looked around him at the motley crew of locals knit together by a single, crazy, ambitious hope. 'Well, we'll never pull it off without Him,' said Valmir, 'and that's the truth.'

Father Ignatius smiled crookedly. 'We beseech thee, God, to bless and prosper this enterprise and forgive the lie we mean to perpetrate to save our homes, our children, and our community. Grant Lord that the *garimpeiros* believe our lie. And grant Lord that wherever we fool the *garimpeiros* into going, they may find the golden consolation of your Love, which is more precious than buried treasure.'

Even after he lowered his hand, the conspirators in the crypt continued to gaze upwards, so transfixed that in the end he felt he had to turn round and see what could possibly be holding their attention.

There, in just the same place that Inez da Souza had sat watching him dig for gold, Honorio Furtado, his boots caked with the mud of the *barrancos*, his hands calloused from digging, sat looking down into the crowded, lighted hole. He must have heard every word.

12

ENOQUE

'Someone come. Someone's gotta come.'

They stared at him: the Enemy, the downfall of all their hopes. He would tell his cronies what was afoot. He would laugh as he told them. Soon their plot would amount to nothing more than a joke in the juice bars, an excuse to show even less respect for the residents of the town and their houses. *You thought you'd trick us into going, did you? Well, let's just see what gold you're keeping hidden under that house of yours, under that store.* The conspirators stared at the yellow-lit face in the open trapdoor. Disembodied by the surrounding darkness, it seemed to hang in mid-air like a golden coin: the face of the Enemy.

'It's my brother,' said Honorio. 'He's real sick.'

'Enoque?' said Maro, and pushed his way through the crowd.

'He's real sick, da Souzzz. It's not just his malaria. I know that. Threw a fit—a real fit, like—foaming and thrashing about. Can't see. Shouldn'ta left him. Didn't wanna leave him, but he made me. Sent me off to Santa Lucia 'bout his eyes. Then I heard you lot . . .'

'You heard us?' said Valmir foolishly.

'Where is Enoque?' asked Ignatius.

'He wanted the boy. Keeps asking for da Souzzz here. But mostly he's seeing monsters. Ghosts and spirits and monsters. Someone's gotta come see. Up at the trailer. By the football.' His voice grew louder in his desperation to break through the cocoon of stillness that gripped the conspirators. 'Well, if you won't, I gotta go. Think more 'bout your houses than people, you do. S'pose you'll be glad when he's dead. Dance on his grave most like.'

'No!' cried Maro, starting up the steps. 'I'll come. The Father'll come. Won't you, Ignatius?'

'Yes, I'll come. But I don't know what I can do. If only there was a clinic. I've always said: if only there was a clinic.' He went to get his white robe and the healing oils and the prayerbook containing the Last Rites, in case it should come to that.

'I'll come,' said Senhora Ferretti, passing The Baby back to its parents. Inez stared at her open-mouthed. Go up to that filthy, derelict trailer in the middle of the *garimpo*? Help a miner? Help that nasty, uncouth Enoque man with his wild animals and his wilder beliefs?

'I'll go to the store. See what I can find,' said Mr da Souza. 'You Furtados were good to me when I needed work.'

'I'll come,' said Valmir.

For Inez, that was the last straw. Help a miner?

'Help a *miner*?' Orlando said out loud, and in the emptying crypt his voice fairly boomed. 'I thought they were the scum we were up against. Help a miner? I wouldn't cross the road to spit on him!'

And when she heard him say the very words she had been thinking, Inez was suddenly hugely glad not to have said them herself. She touched Orlando gently on the sleeve. 'But this isn't any old miner, you see? This is Enoque.' For in her head she could see a sunlit street through the cords of a hammock, tufts of dust chasing each other down the road, her father smoking his one cigar of the day while the Furtado brothers lounged on the boardwalk steps of the store saying how it would be when they were rich. And the tayra slept in Enoque's dirty hat.

The great sodden blanket of heat which precedes the rainy season had already settled over the houses and *barrancos*. Every window stood open, its netting rattling at the onslaught of a million flying insects. The timber of houses hanging over the chasm groaned with the strain of staying upright. The stench of the *garimp* latrines enveloped the town, trapped beneath an invisible ceiling of stale, hot air. It was as if the year were used up and soiled: time to throw it away and begin again.

Not even Honorio's fright prepared them for the sight that awaited them in the Furtado trailer. Here was the palace of the *desbravadors* of Vazia. The floor was a crisp, choppy brown with layers of mud walked in off the *barrancos*. The shelves and sills were alive with cockroaches. Under a pile of blankets, without any sheets, Enoque lay in his boots and jeans and vest, his arms crossed over his face. More than the cockroaches were the evil spirits Enoque knew to be besieging his bed. He greeted their arrival with screams of, 'The *Hekura*! They're fighting over me! Feel how they're shaking the van!' The van did shake considerably as Senhora Ferretti squeezed her way through the small, metal door, but Enoque insisted it was the *Hekura's* doing. They looked to Honorio for a translation.

'Spirits. Good and bad,' he said pulling his brother's blankets into fewer creases and knots.

'I think it's the Good on that side and the Bad over there,' cried Enoque pleadingly, and his brother shut the windows on the side attacked by the evil *Hekura*. 'But I don't know!' wailed Enoque, and his brother shut all the windows, just to be sure. For a moment Enoque was pacified.

'I brought the da Souzzz kids and the singing lady,' said Honorio, knowing which names would please most.

'You brought the singing lady here? La Samba Senhora? You shouldn't oughta brung a lady like that to a place like this. Not a lady like that.'

Senhora Ferretti, immobile until then with a mixture of revulsion and embarrassment at how her huge bulk filled the caravan, suddenly came to life. 'Heat some water and let's clean this fellow up,' she said.

'We're outa butane,' said Honorio helplessly.

'So? Did Prometheus steal butane from Mount Olympus? Did the Almighty divide night from day and illumine them with butane?' He goggled at her, his lips trembling slightly. 'I mean have you lost the art of building a good, old-fashioned *fire?*' she stormed at him, and he fled the trailer in search of firewood.

'Did you see it out there, Maro?' Enoque called out, without turning his head. 'I can't see. It's my eyes. I can hear it. Reckon I heard it. But I can't see, see? Did you see it, coming here?'

'See what, Mr Furtado, sir?'

'The *chonchon*. I have to fight him soon, see? I never fought no one with my eyes shut before.'

'I didn't see anything, Enoque. What does it look like? We'll fight it for you! Won't we?' he appealed to his sister.

She could neither speak nor think. She moved backwards until she was pressed up against Father Ignatius. Why did he not speak? Why did he not put Enoque right— tell him that these monsters of his did not exist? Only God and the saints and the angels existed—and her dad coming with some medicine.

'Human head. Big ears,' said Enoque. 'Ears big as wings. Uses them to fly round looking out for sick folk. Probably flying round outside. Calling me out. To fight it. Listen!' They listened. They could not help but listen. The panels of the caravan ticked, cooling after the day's heat. The claws of the tayra and the monkey scrabbled on the metal shelves where they perched at night. The night insects collided with the caravan, chasing reflections of the moon.

Whoomph.

Outside, Honorio cursed as he lit a campfire with a paraffin-soaked rag. It lit more readily than he expected. Everyone in the caravan jumped out of their wits.

'Anyone got any ideas,' said Senhora Ferretti in a businesslike way.

'Mercury poisoning, I think,' said Valmir. For once in his life he sounded uncertain. 'Convulsions, blindness. You've lost the feeling in your hands and feet lately, haven't you, Mr Furtado? I've seen his hands shake, too. They used to call it the Hatter's Shake. Because hatters used mercury to shine top hats. It's why they went mad, too. You know? Mad hatters?' This completely gratuitous piece of general knowledge hung in the air. No one who was there that night ever forgot it: that hatters used mercury once to shine top hats. No one there had ever seen a top hat, met a hatter; it would never be useful; it would never be relevant. And yet there it stuck, as permanently fixed as their three-times table or the date of Christmas Day, because of where and when they had heard it.

'If it wins, it gets to drink my blood, see?' said Enoque, raising himself up on his elbows. 'In at the throat—that's the death rattle—then it can drink my blood.'

'There's no such thing as a *chonchon*, Enoque!' cried Inez. 'Really and truly! I wouldn't lie to you!' But Enoque had told many lies in his life, so he knew one when he heard one. He knew the *chonchon* existed, because he had lived for long periods of time with Indians who also knew that the *chonchon* existed. Just as Inez knew the saints watched over her because she had lived all her life among good, devout Catholics. 'Tell him, Father! Tell him there's no such thing!'

Enoque gave a groan of such fright and horror and pain that the *chonchon's* breath clouded the window glass and made it, too, sweat. There were wistiti monkeys clambering on the roof, eating food scraps from the rubbish heaps. Their claws scratched on the metalwork. Enoque arched his back and clenched his teeth and his knees swung to and fro in uncontrollable convulsions, tossing his blanket on to the floor. It looked exactly as if he were wrestling with an invisible monster, his hands scrabbling futilely for a grip on some smooth, scaly, lizardly opponent.

As the convulsion came to an end, Father Ignatius seemed suddenly to wake from a deep sleep. He moved Inez out of his way and crouched down beside the bunk, his white skirts spreading around him as if he were a snowman melting in the suffocating heat. 'Listen to me, Enoque. Can you hear me? Listen. You recall how the farmers in the Nordeste cure their animals?'

'Yes,' said Enoque. 'No.'

'How they draw a magic circle round a cow, say, that's sick? And pray to Saint Barbara?'

'Yes, yes! A magic circle! I'd be safe there, wouldn't I? Nothing could get to me!'

'And we could all pray to Santa Barbara,' the priest persisted, insinuating different pictures, different memories into a mind molten with fever and fright.

The suggestion trickled through Enoque's brain, as corrosive and bright as the mercury that had poisoned it. 'Santa Lucia, she weren't no good. But Barbara now: she could keep off the *chonchon*, I reckon, if she wanted. Prayed to her once, and we whipped Belem in the League Cup. Scored from thirty yards out, I did. The saints've been good to me, it's true.'

The heat in the caravan increased with every new raincloud that piled itself on Serra Vazia like a clod of earth. Ignatius was anxious to get the sick man out in the open air, out of the dirty oven where they all seemed to be stewing. To do that, he had to wrestle the idea of the *chonchon* out of Enoque's imagination. It is a waste of time simply to rubbish what a man devoutly believes. So Ignatius used one magic to drive out another.

By everyone taking a hold of the underblanket, they were able to lift Enoque and carry him clumsily outside. Honorio leapt up from beside the fire, looking up at the sky as if the *chonchon* would at any moment swoop down on its prey. 'What you doing? Where you taking him?'

A crack of dry lightning lit up the scenery between the *garimpeiros'* tents and trailers. It showed how the

120

white centre spot of the football pitch had been left untouched by their digging. (After all, for a Brazilian, it would have been virtual sacrilege to sink a spade through such a mark.) So it was to the kick-off spot of Serra Vazia FC that Enoque's friends carried him—to its luminous whiteness freshly painted during the first hopeful days of prosperity. The paint was even in evidence— a chalky bucket set hard like plaster of Paris, which needed reviving with hot water. Then, using their hands and shoes, and in the best traditions of superstitious cattle farmers, they daubed a magic circle around Enoque Furtado.

Only Valmir held off, appalled by such foolishness, confirmed in his worst opinions of Christianity. Just when he thought he had chanced upon a fellow intellectual in Ignatius, here he was—a man of good education— crawling about a football pitch daubing white slurry round a dying man. His robes dragged through the line he had already drawn. Was that why priests wore white? So as to be ready to indulge in this kind of mumbo jumbo?

In completing the circle, Ignatius collided with Inez and splattered her with white paint. They were breathless with the exertion, sweltering in the heat. They leaned against one another for a moment to recover. He stumbled a little in getting to his feet, unaccustomed to wearing a robe outside the precincts of the church.

At the centre of the magic circle Enoque Furtado lay in the throes of mercury poisoning aggravated by malaria. Now and then what he said made sense. Now and then he believed himself buried alive in the graves of the Incan Indians he had once plundered for gold as a *wakeiro*. Their angry ghosts berated him with the theft of their gravegoods.

La Senhora took the bowl of clean, hot water Honorio brought, and bathed his face, telling him that the circle was complete, praying in a whisper to Santa Barbara. Once he was persuaded of the circle's existence, once the water cooling on his face brought his fever down a degree or two, he became a lot calmer, and lay still. 'Where else would she be right now, right?' he observed in a soft, singing voice. 'Where else would that Barbara woman be, if she's not in among us miners, eh?'

'That's right,' said Senhora Ferretti. 'Where else.'

'Though it's a hell of a place for a lady.'

'She must be used to it. And this is surely preferable to curing sick cows. However, we mustn't detain her for too long, must we?'

His sky was empty of *chonchons*, his soul was no longer required to wrestle with demon monsters. Drops of rain, sparse as morning dew, came at the time of dewfall. They woke Enoque who had fallen into a deep, dreamless sleep, and he opened his eyes and saw—SAW! (through one eye at least), his brother and friends dozing round the perimeter of a white chalk circle in the grass. 'She's a good woman, that Barbara,' he said loudly, to catch their attention. 'That Santa Lucia, too. I done her wrong thinking she didn't answer no prayers.'

They jumped up and ran to him, scuffing gaps in the magic circle. Inez washed his face with cool water, and Maro fetched the monkey and tayra from the trailer to sit on Enoque's stomach within reach of his hands. The bout of malaria was on the wane. The symptoms of the mercurial poisoning subsided, granted him a remission, at least. The adults withdrew, seeing that Enoque was with his favourite companions: children and animals.

'If only there was a clinic inside a hundred miles . . .' said Father Ignatius to Valmir, knowing that there, at least, they were bound to agree. He felt that the night had distanced the student from his circle of friends—shut him out of their circle as surely as the magic chalkdust had shut out Enoque's imagined demons.

'You'll have to pray to Santa Barbara for one then, won't you?' Valmir retorted snidely. 'Then maybe a doctor or two will come floating down from the sky.'

Ignatius looked him in the eye, unapologetic. 'Everyone makes God in his own image, Val,' he said. 'We think ours likes poetry and books, and reads the political columns in the newspapers.'

'*Ours*? Leave me out of it,' said Valmir, but Ignatius went on anyway.

'Is our Divine Intellectual any more sensible a picture to paint than Enoque's skyful of angelic football supporters fighting a zooful of monsters and ghouls? We're all only making a wild stab at it.'

Valmir looked him up and down with a sneer of contempt, the muddy white robe, the T-shirt commemorating the Pope's visit, the hair raised into white spikes where he had run chalky hands through it. 'Well, someone's god had best come up with a miracle to save Vazia. 'Cos our plans have gone down the toilet, and that's for sure.'

'You really think so? I'm sure you're wrong . . . And don't talk to the priest like that.' Senhora Ferretti thrust a tin mug of sludge-black coffee between them, presenting it to Ignatius. 'Disrespectful delinquent,' she snarled at Valmir.

Ignatius burned himself on the cup and did not even notice. 'You mean Honorio *didn't* hear what we were saying last night?' he asked La Senhora, dropping his voice to a whisper.

'Oh, he heard well enough. I asked him this morning.'

'You asked him? Straight out?'

'I believe in being direct,' she replied. 'Anyway, he doesn't think our plan to make the *garimps* move on will work. But he's prepared to present the notion to his brother, as soon as Enoque is feeling better.'

'What notion?' asked Valmir open-mouthed.

'The notion of helping us, of course,' said La Senhora. 'I suppose you want a cup of coffee too, do you, you rude boy?'

123

'Brother Enoque,' said Honorio. 'These people want the miners to clear off. They're thinking to put it about that there's another strike. Up country. A phoney *fofoca*, like. To draw us *garimps* off, see? Won't work, will it? Can they make it work, d'you think?'

Enoque sat up in the bunk, tucked up between clean sheets, his head looking gaunt and old against clean pillows. Mrs da Souza had brought them from the store, and scrubbed the place clean. It smelled now of disinfectant and air fresheners—a scent which terrified the animals. Outside, the tayra went from wheel to wheel of the trailer, leaving its musk, reclaiming its territory.

Enoque felt like a king. Even in his days as *desbravador*, he had never slept between sheets. He gazed around him, renewing his acquaintance with tin walls he had forgotten were cream: he had come to think of them as striped plush with green mould. 'Nope. Won't work,' he said categorically. 'You ain't got the cash, none of you. How you gonna play at *bamburrados* without no cash to splash about? You'd be the worst ones to do it, too. Seeing how you hate gold, deep down. Never understood 'bout that. What you got against it? Never understood that. Don't seem to see her for the beauty she is. Look.' He rooted about inside his shirt, but his fingertips were numb, nerveless, unserviceable. Maro had to help him extricate a golden brooch worn on a length of chewed ribbon round his neck. 'Found it in a grave up Guyana way. Incan Indian it is. Look at it.' He held it up on the palm of his hand. The hand shook so much that the brooch jumped about as though it were alive. But they could see the intricate delicacy of its design. Circles broke in a splash which were then crossed through, as if by a fish's fin splitting the ripples.

'It's like a treble clef,' said Senhora Ferretti.

'Can't rust. Can't spoil. Thousand years and more it lay in a dirty hole with a dead man. Dead man's up and gone. Justa spirit now somewhere in the hills. But this: it's like the day it was made. And think of the work that went in, eh? Father teaching his son, teaching his son, teaching his. On and on. Passing down the art. How to bend it to a thought that's only in your head in the morning and there it is in your hand by nightfall. How to make something like this. Out a rock. Out a piece of dirt. Diamonds the same: only be coal, they would, if those dinosaurs hadn'ta stomped down so hard with their big feet—packed the ground hard.'

'My brother had a yen to be a goldsmith,' explained Honorio unnecessarily. All eyes rested on the twist of Incan gold trembling in a hand weakened by its lifelong pursuit of gold.

'But you and Honorio, you'd at least keep our secret, Enoque?' said Senhora Ferretti. 'If we do give it a try? You needn't give us away to the other *garimpeiros*.'

'Please, Enoque,' said Valmir. 'The rains are coming any day. The whole place will come down like a house of cards. Slide into the hole. We have to try something.'

'*Please*, Enoque,' said Mr da Souza. 'No one's getting rich but the fat cats. Even you. You've found nothing worth a mention.'

'Please, Enoque,' said Inez. 'If all the *garimps* were like you, we wouldn't want them to go.'

'Please, Enoque,' said Maro. 'I know you've lived everywhere, and everywhere you go is home and every bit of ground's just somewhere to dig for you, but I've never had nowhere else. It's home and I like it and I don't want it to fall down and have to sleep in a tree, though I wouldn't mind sleeping in a tree if I had somewhere to go home to after and see the light coming out the window and say how it was and then go to bed properly. Here. In my house.'

Enoque suddenly grinned, showing a set of teeth stained by tobacco. 'A photo! That's what it needs. That gap there. Now it's clean. It needs a photo!' He turned a hopeful and appealing face towards Senhora Ferretti. 'You got such a thing, Senhora? From your days in the theatre? You got a picture portrait of you?'

'I was never in the theatre, Mr Furtado.'

'Still. You got a photo, I know. Handsome woman like you.' He broke off, aware of a certain unanswered question hanging in the air, looking out of the faces around him. They did not seem to appreciate the happiness a photograph would bring him. 'Well, *'course* I won't give you away to the *garimps*. What d'you take me for? Help you best I can, 'course I will! Can help you get the Indians away for a start, can't we, Honorio? Can get the Indians to clear off the river and go. Don't know about the rest. Not without the cash. We ain't got it, Honorio and me, just like usual.' He sighed resignedly. 'I'll have to have a think, and I'm not too hot at thinking right now. But you see here,' he added sternly. 'From now on what you people says is what I go along with. Right? What? If it wasn't for you people, I'd be out there now. The *noreshi* gone out of me. Running loose in the forest. My soul inside some animal, if it weren't for you good people.'

Valmir looked sidelong at Ignatius, just as Ignatius looked sidelong at him. Neither could refrain from a grin. Then a snicker grew to a splutter and a splutter to a great noisy uproarious mirth, as student and priest leant against each other crying with laughter. 'Enoque Furtado, you're an incorrigible pantheistical heathen!' howled Ignatius, the chalk in his hair rising in clouds round his head.

'Thank you very much, Father, I'm sure,' said Enoque proudly, and, with the tayra sitting on the top of his head, he looked for all the world like Davy Crocket before the Alamo.

13

THE DAY OF THE DEAD

There are live, flesh-and-fur horrors enough in the night jungle without adding supernatural ones. And yet why should there not be monsters and spirits, too? Huge bull-dog bats plunge out of the trees to snatch live fish from the river. Peccary boars with tusks sharp as shrapnel burst like shells through the clearings. Vile, faceless sloths hang in the branches, their fur green with algae and a-flicker with infestations of moth, hunted by coral snakes of black, yellow, and red. Pitcher flowers open their stinking petals to lure flies into their poisonous stomachs. Capybara, like guinea pigs grown to the size of hogs, rootle among fleshy fungi which smell of death. Why then should there not be *chonchons* hunting the souls of dying men, or good and evil *hekura* swimming invisible through the sweltering air. Why should the giant inia not turn itself, as legend said, into a woman with long silken hair and go searching the banks for a mate to kiss and draw down into the river? Why should there not be, as the Indians believed, a great serpent goddess called *Boiuna*, her eyes shining like lanterns, changing at will into a phantom ship, mooring at night to take on board human flesh? Why not the *curupira* spirit, protecting the trees from senseless destruction, destroying the enemies of the trees? Why should there not be such phenomena? Especially on The Day of the Dead.

'It makes itself to look like some little Indian boy running 'bout hither and yon, grinning at you with green teeth. Yeah, green teeth. And it walks backwards, so as if you sees it coming, you thinks as it's going, and if you sees it going you thinks it a-coming. It likes to fool a body, see, the *curupira*.' Enoque described the Indian spirits as

127

though he were describing any real-life bird or monkey: descriptions untinged by disbelief. And yet he thought nothing of dressing Maro up, disguising him with weed for hair and dyeing his whole body and face red with *urucu* oil. He stained the boy's teeth green with tobacco leaves, and taught him how to frighten the Indians.

The tobacco juice made Maro sick and dizzy. The weed dangled down cold and slimy on to his shoulders, and strands kept slithering away down his back like lizards. Inez looked him up and down dubiously. She was of the opinion they should have bribed a real Indian boy to imitate the *curupira*, but Enoque said that Maro would do just fine.

'Soon see,' Inez said darkly, and returned to refurbishing the chicken wire dinosaur. It was the one which had stood for so many years jammed between the stationery cupboard and book locker in her classroom. In all the years it had overshadowed her education, she had never thought it would play such a vital role in her life. Now the idea was to lash it to a raft and float it downriver in the hope that the superstitious Indians would mistake it for the snake goddess *Boiuna* and run for their lives.

The paper beast had been in good fettle when it left the school, but while fetching it down, in secret, as far as the *barrancos*, several scales had dropped off and someone's hand had gone through its throat, so that it looked like the victim of shooting at close range. There was no point in mending it: in the dark it would pass muster; in the dark it would just about do. She did push the hilts of two torches through the big saucer eyes made of tinfoil—it made a noise like piercing a new jar of coffee—and experimented, turning on the switches. The torches lolled unevenly in their sockets, one looking up into the sky, one staring downwards. 'Will this really work?' she asked.

But it was no use asking Enoque. He believed in everything—in Marabá FC winning the World Cup, in finding diamonds or gold enough to make him a millionaire, in wing-eared spirits drinking his blood, and in river monsters fearful enough to frighten away whole tribes of Indians. His brother was hardly any better. It was he who accompanied the children down to the River Xingu.

In order to reach the river, brother and sister had to climb inside the dinosaur and walk with it over their heads, as rowers carry a skiff. They could see out through the hole in the throat, and various missing scales. The oval hoop from which the legs and tail dangled harnessed Inez and Maro together in tandem, and if she tumbled, he was pulled off balance too. When he slipped, she caught her breath. Honorio walked ahead, picking a safe path between the *barrancos*. He would not have chosen to pass by the graveyard, but all the other routes to the river were impassable to a three-metre dinosaur. The weed of Maro's hair snagged on the chicken wire. He felt like a mermaid caught in a lobster pot. He dreaded passing by the graveyard, too—tonight of all nights—but did not want to admit to his fright in front of Honorio and his sister. It had to be done.

Any other year, the burial ground would have been alive with lights and activity. The Day of the Dead was a day to dress the graves of dead grandfathers, mothers, uncles with flowers and lights, *chope* beer or manioc liquor. Not so this December. Amilcar's grave was certainly piled high with flowers, which glowed whitely in the dark, as though light were springing up from underground. A few other graves had been stuck with candles, but there was a stiff, hot breeze of the kind that preceeds the Big Rain, and all the flames had blown out, leaving the wax stalks to poke out of the earth like single skeletal fingers. It was a day when even Christian Catholics were open to the thought of Christian relations rising up and dancing on their coffins. Given the plight of Serra Vazia, it did not seem unreasonable that whole tribes of ghosts should clamber out of their graves howling with protest at the fate of their town.

129

Glimpsing all this ahead of her, Inez came to an abrupt halt in front of Maro and he banged into her. 'I'm not going by there,' she hissed. Maro was relieved that she had been the one to say it. The graveyard mounted up on their right like Golgotha. Such deep *barrancos* had been dug on all four sides of it that sheer escarpments of mud rose up now—escarpments behind which the dead lay sleeping. It was no longer possible to think of them as *under* the ground, for the ground around had been scraped away. They were simply contained within a mound, a sandcastle which might at any moment subside and spill its contents across the path where Inez and Maro were walking. Honorio did not hear Inez call out to him in a whisper. She could have shouted, and Honorio would still have mistaken it for the cry of a *hekura* or the flight of the *chonchon*. He was just as enveloped in the horrors of the night and of their surroundings.

What was that sticking out of the escarpment? A tree root? Yes, a tree root. It had to be. What was that noise? A howler monkey? Yes, a monkey. It had to be. Inside the dinosaur, the joint heat of their bodies made Inez and Maro gently melt, their faces grizzling sweat, their cotton shirts sticking to them like the skin off hot milk. No one granted them permission to chicken out. So they were obliged to shuffle on past the graveyard. Finally they collided with the forest edge where creepers trailed dangling cords over the dinosaur's back, and tubers tripped them at every step.

Amilcar's mother had told them to use the *balsa* her son had been using when he drowned; she said it would be a comfort to her if the raft served to empty Serra Vazia of miners, seeming to blame them somehow for her son's drowning. But it was one thing to think of mounting the dinosaur on the raft and another to do it. Maro could not go beyond the river bank without spoiling his painted disguise. So Honorio took his place. The riverbed was slippery; they staggered and slithered without being able to see. The model trailed its tissue ribcage in the water, and scales turned to pulp and drifted away into a darkness which began inside their chicken wire shell and continued all the way to Mars.

All the valuable machinery had been removed which had once kept the *balsa* stable. It tipped up and skidded away from them as they tried to climb aboard. But finally they succeeded, Inez and Honorio, in wrestling the dilapidated dinosaur aboard and propping it over what remained of the machine mountings. Inez crawled aboard herself and lit the torch eyes. They squinted weakly down the river, a short-sighted paper dragon more comical than fearsome. She found herself thinking: this is like the Independence Day parade all over again: me in the middle of it, puny and useless—only good for laughing at—bits of paper and wire, when everyone else has steel and gold. She resented Honorio already for making her a laughing stock among the Indians. She was just thinking this when he set her adrift, and the raft circled slowly on the river before picking up speed on the current.

She was lying on her face, concealed beneath a disused dinosaur, her head towards the stern, steering the raft with its single oar. The dangling paper legs of the beast streamed out of all four corners of the raft, disintegrating quickly as though its meat were melting down to the bone in the boiling current. Too late to call a halt to the night's work, she glimpsed her brother standing on the river bank, the fright and uncertainty plain enough on his face even through all that darkness. Why were the grown-ups not doing this? The grown-ups should be doing it. Of course, none of them would pass for a dwarf Indian sprite, and none of them could have curled up and hidden on the little raft. She had a sudden picture of Senhora Ferretti attempting it, and began to giggle, her nervousness catching at her breath until she was hiccuping with laughter. 'Who'll see me, in any case?' she whispered up at the squinting monster. 'Who's going to see us? Bet there isn't an Indian for miles around!' That made her feel better—even though it did mean she was doing it all for nothing. And there was still the problem of how to get back to shore when the charade was over.

Watching his sister from the bank, Maro realized that the time had come for him to play his part—to become the *curupira*, guardian spirit of the trees. Instead he felt small and sick and useless. The whole idea was preposterous. For one thing, how was anyone supposed to know that his teeth were green? If one of the Indians got close enough to see, they would recognize him plainly for the boy at the general store with weed on his head and a loincloth in place of his trousers. (How was it that the native boys could wear a loincloth with such ease when his slipped down continually over his hip bones like one of The Baby's nappies? It was damp with sweat, too.) He wished Inez had not insisted so very hard that she and he were the only ones capable of working the trick. Surely a grown-up would have been better—braver?

The perfumes and noises of the forest increased as the daylight decreased. The *pium* flies gathered over the last reflected light of the water. The animals came out to drink. A smell of wood smoke travelled the air like the soul of a dead tree. Somewhere the forest was burning, being burned. Perhaps the smoke had come to sympathize with the fate of its fellow trees around Serra Vazia. Gouged up by the high pressure hoses, their roots washed bare, they lay about him now, arthritic and crippled and dying, their last few leaves curled into false, golden fruit. An insect fell out of the trees on to his shoulder. The only sky visible was lousy with bulldog bats.

Unlike his sister, he had no trouble at all believing in spirits and ghouls. What if the Serpent Goddess took offence at Inez's impersonation? What if he were to meet the real *curupira*—here—on this very forest path? Would it chase him through the forest, leading him astray to lose him in the heart of trackless jungle to be eaten by boa constrictors or soldier ants? He decided he would go home and tell his father: not on the Festival of the Dead. Any other night but not on the Night of the Dead. Maro turned round—and found that in the darkness, without the crack of a twig or the disturbing of a monkey, three figures had arrived at his back.

Three Indians, their faces crossed through with a band of paint across the cheeks and nose, stood with their thumbs hooked in the strings of their bows. They opened their mouths—to laugh at him, he supposed, or to snarl. Maro did not stay to see which. As he backed away from them, he saw only the rotten stumps of their teeth, then he turned and started to run—tripping over tree roots, colliding with sharp, fleshy plants. They could undoubtedly run faster than he. Or perhaps even now they were taking aim with bow and arrow, outraged at the insult to their religion. In any case, he had better dodge and dart, try to lose himself among the motley of shadow and bushes, hide rather than try to outrun them. He scrabbled under a fallen tree, leaving his loincloth caught on a splinter of bark. He wormed between two anthills, and left his weedy hair dangling from a bird's nest. The white monkeys hooted with joy at his predicament, swinging down to geek at him with upside-down faces and five hands to his two. He could not hear the Indians following him—and concluded they must certainly be ghosts, in which case there was no point in running. He came to a halt. If they were *curupira*, they would *want* him to run in panic and lose himself in the forest, and then he would never see his friends or family again. Not his mother nor the general store nor his photograph of Pele nor the football pennants tied to his hammock ropes. That thought alone made him stop dead and turn round.

The three figures were still silhouetted against the light of the river. They had started after him but not come far. One pointed a finger towards him—or was he casting a spell? Maro turned to run again, slipped off the river bank into shallow water, and his knee brushed against a round mound of ground which flinched and shuddered and roused up and crashed against him. The inia belly-flopped into the deep water. Maro heard the wash from the impact swamp the hollow tree roots with a glop-glop. Then the big flippers of the inia pumped away downstream, in the direction Inez had gone, turning the glossy water to a hissing foam, leaving its oblique footprints in the river to slowly melt away. Somewhere a snake hissed derisively at Maro's babyish fright. Then his bare toes crashed against a piece of brick, and he found himself running over land sprinkled with masonry. He was among the coping stones of the rubber factory chimney, whose fall had pitched them as far as the forest's edge.

By the time he had picked his way over the *barrancos* to the store, he had recovered his breath and stopped crying. So his mother saw nothing but a naked boy standing in the doorway with nothing at all to say for himself. She shouted at him for leaving his sister behind: '*Where is she? You mean to say you've left her out there? On the river? Alone?*' And she lashed out at him with slapping hands. When he did not dodge away or duck the blows, she realized instantly the state of his heart, and with the noise of the slaps still singing and their shape still stinging, she drew his face against her apron and wrapped him round in a bathtowel from the pile on the sofa. The Baby was sitting between a yawning gap in the floorboards, filtering dry semolina through the decorative holes in Mr da Souza's straw hat.

Floating downstream, intent on steering the clumsy raft, Inez heard a rhythmic splash, splash, splash in the river behind her. She did not think of inias, nor of crocodiles, nor catfish, nor anaconda, nor capybara. She thought only of the Serpent Goddess *Boiuna* who could make herself into a ship and sail the river searching for human prey.

134

Inez prayed to the saints, but what saint in his right mind would come here in his long white gown and bare white feet? Saints inhabited still, solid buildings of white stone, under roofs of corrugated silver tin, not this slipping wet world writhing with vegetation, snakes and fish, swarming with beetles and spiders and ants. The very sap of the flowers was venomous sweet.

She tried to use the paddle to increase her speed, but she only set the raft rocking violently. Class Three's dinosaur lunged this way and that, and dropped one eye in the river: Inez saw it shine and bubble below the water as she was swept over the sinking torch. The noise of the Goddess's ship closed on her in the darkness: it was going to ram her, to sink her, to rend her and the wire dragon into shapeless litter and tissuey pulp. There was a thump, and one corner of the raft was lifted clear out of the water with such an upheaval that Inez was thrown on to her back, and the dinosaur plunged its nose into the stream. The *balsa* was set spinning by the collision—round and round, round and round, yawing and pitching, so that a film of water washed all over its length in a blood-warm surge. Inez closed her eyes and inwardly apologized to her mother for dying so young.

Then the raft came to a sudden halt which detached Inez from the rudder oar and sped her down all the slippery length of the hollow dinosaur to spew her off the front of the raft into shallow water. The roots of a mangrove tree had captured the *balsa*, and the clambering complication of its roots snatched the dinosaur by its neck and rended him clear off the raft, buckling body and neck into one chicken wire entanglement.

Inez seemed to have sailed so far that it would not have surprised her to find herself in Manaus, or down by the sea. But as she stood, wetly hysterical, on a crescent of muddy riverbank, she recognized, little by little, a spot where she and Maro had often come to fish in the old days. Sure enough, when she turned round, the lights of the *garimpeiro* camp on the football pitch were glimmering at her through a pallisade of trees.

Enoque Furtado came hurrying along the bank, hopping and stumbling, lamed by mud and roots as much as disability. 'You all right, missus?' he asked. The creepers he had run through clung to his chest and legs and made him look like some centipedal native god or a jungle plant come to life.

'Is Maro okay? Tell Maro he needn't do this if he doesn't want to,' was the first thing she said.

'He's done. He done good,' said Enoque panting with exertion. 'You both done real good.'

In the morning, a whole tract of riverbank was totally empty. The Indian calling at the store to buy manioc flour for his journey said that *Boiuna*, the Serpent Goddess, had been seen the night before.

'I heard something about that,' said Mr da Souza cautiously. 'Saw it, did you?'

Not he, but one of his kin had heard from certain of their kin that the children had been talking among themselves of seeing a monster in the river the previous night. Some even said it was not an Indian who had seen it first, but a Christian *garimp*. Whoever had begun it, the rumour had soon spread among the Indians panning the river and traipsing between Vazia and the riverbank with their copper bowls. Evil magic and bad omens. Mr da Souza did nothing to discourage the rumours. He even mentioned that a *curupira* had been spoken of too, by someone in his shop.

'We heard that also!' cried the Indian, his eyes widening. 'Childs of ours. Mothers, fathers say they talking big— making big story. But *shaman* he ask them straight, and they answer pretty damn good.'

The Indian children had been judged not to be lying, by the tribal magic man. The *curupira* had tried to lead them

136

into the forest, they said—to lose them—first running away, then turning round to lure them on, then ducking out of sight. It had weed on its head, so they supposed it had been swimming. If their description had been more traditionally correct, the *shaman* would have believed them less: only liars are accurate.

This judgement by the *shaman* had been crucial in deciding the Indians to move away. The forest was huge: it held hardships and rewards enough for forty lifetimes. Without the approval of their gods and the co-operation of the spirit world, Serra Vazia became, overnight, one of the least inviting few acres to inhabit. The Indian left the general store in such a hurry that he forgot his manioc flour and had to come back. As the door closed behind him a second time, a little of the guilt slid from Mr da Souza's shoulders. Ever since he helped to encourage the rumours of gold beneath Main Street in the hope of better trade, he had felt personally responsible for the disaster suffered by the town. Now at least he had done something to make the newcomers go away—even though the bulk remained, and it would take more than rumours of monsters and spirits to shift them.

'It worked!' cried Maro, and the bad memories of that night were erased like chalk from a blackboard. 'We did it! We fooled them!'

Inez said nothing, too ashamed to recount—and yet unable to stop believing—that *Boiuna*, Serpent Goddess of the Xingu, had brushed against her raft in the early hours of the Night of the Dead.

Ever since the fire, Senhora Ferretti had formed a special attachment for The Baby. They would go for perilous walks together, skirting the *barrancos* to reach La Senhora's apartment where The Baby would sort and sift her beads and buttons in an endless geological assay. Now and then, things would be filched away for some secret collection—

the occasional black-eyed bean or broken cup-handle. So it was not unusual for the teacher to open a box and find its contents strangely re-organized.

In preparation for Proclamation of the Republic Day, she was making meat pies, her faded blue dress covered by an apron big as a sail. The Baby played behind her with the opening pedal bin.

Once La Senhora had been in the habit of making two pies to eat in the respectable loneliness of her spinster flat, pouring herself a small glass of apricot liqueur while she cooked, and another while she ate. This year she would make twenty pies and entertain all the conspirators to one last grand patriotic party before her apartment succumbed to its inevitable fate. It would be like a cocktail party on the poop of the Titanic, and the thought brought a surge of emotion to her breast, which was not altogether un-pleasant. With a grand flourish she sprinkled the canister of manioc flour over the kitchen worktop where she meant to roll out the pastry.

She was accustomed to finding weevils or ants in the flour. She was not used to it glittering. She poked about at it, leaving her big fingerprints in the white and gold. A single ant ploughed its way across the snowy, glittering landscape towards a mountain of dough.

'Child. Did you put something in here?' La Senhora asked. The Baby glanced at the worktop and went back to playing. 'Where did you find it?' The Baby, given its age, did not reply.

Senhora Ferretti wiped her fingers, took off her apron, poured a larger-than-usual apricot liqueur, and took The Baby for a walk while the thought of the flour canister was still fresh in its infant mind. The walk led, as it usually did, to the hole where The Baby had been found the morning after the Fire. La Senhora, being an amateur psychologist, had always supposed the child to be working out the horrors of that night, in going there. Now she began to have other ideas.

138

Senhora Ferretti took The Baby next to the Church of Santa Barbara and told Father Ignatius about the flour shaker, about their little expedition and what they had found. She said, when she had finished, 'I had better show Mr and Mrs da Souza. I don't know what made me come here first. It's their baby who found it, after all.'

'Ask Maro and Inez first. They might react differently from their parents,' said Ignatius.

So Senhora Ferretti waited until she saw one or other of the children away from the store. The opportunity did not arise until the mid-week Mass, after which both priest and teacher converged on Inez da Souza.

'Something has happened, Inez,' said La Senhora. 'Before I tell you what it is, would you answer me a question?'

'Of course, Senhora.'

'What would your . . . what do you suppose . . . how do you think your father and mother would react if they came into some money.'

'How much?' said Inez.

'Enough to buy another store. Somewhere else.'

'Then they'd buy a store somewhere else,' said Inez.

'Would they help the town to get rid of the miners?' asked Ignatius. 'Think hard now. Would they?'

Inez thought hard. Not that the question was difficult to answer, but the answer sounded disloyal. 'If they had millions they'd help the miners. I'm sure they would. But first they'd buy a store somewhere else. To be on the safe side. Dad likes to live on the safe side. He has us to think about.'

'What about *you*? What would *you* do?' said Senhora Ferretti.

Inez looked up at her. A month ago she would have thrown the teacher's words back at her: 'Get out of here. That's what we all want, isn't it? To get out of here?' But now they were fellow conspirators, and how could that fellowship continue if she did not abide by the rules of the club? 'We all want to save the town,' she said . . . and thought how priggish it sounded. 'Maro would buy a bike,' she thought aloud, letting her imagination drift. 'Maybe I would, too. Before anything.'

'You can do that,' said Father Ignatius fetching out a bank roll seemingly big enough to finance another visit by the Pope. 'I'll get you a bike each . . . If you'll let me use the rest to save the town.'

They took her aside into the chapel of Santa Lucia. Enoque's carved eyeball still rested between the saint's carved feet. Perhaps Lucia had done the best she could: Enoque had the sight back in one eye at least. There in the side-chapel, Senhora Ferretti told Inez how The Baby, on the night of the fire, finding itself lost in dangerous and frightening surroundings far from home, had done what it could to make a warm nest. Finding the Fixer's llama-wool coat, scorched and singed but not burning, The Baby had dragged it over to a little hole half-filled with rubble, and curled up inside it, emerging only at the sound of frantic searching and familiar voices. The coat had been over-looked in the joy of finding the child.

Return visits to the secret den had unearthed, from the various pouches of the Fixer's coat-lining, 5,000 American dollars, 600 Brazilian cruzeiros, twelve ounces of gold-dust and a bunch of silver keys. All except for the keys, the pretty silver keys, The Baby was prepared to part with in return for sweets, a beany cap, and the Senhora's own orange samba maracas.

'Valmir and I, we'll go to Marabá,' said Father Ignatius. 'Pass ourselves off as *bamburrados*—pretend we've really struck it big. Flash this money about. Cash in the gold-dust. That's what Enoque told us would work. Talk about some big strike up north. Start a real *fofoca* . . . If you say we can use The Baby's . . . good fortune that way.'

'Rightly we should hand it all back to the Fixer,' said La Senhora. 'It's his property, the little rat.'

'No!' Inez did not know what she felt, but it was not the smallest inclination to give the Fixer back his coat. 'Rightly we should tell Mum and Dad.'

'Yes,' agreed both teacher and priest, casting all the moral burden squarely and unfairly back on to Inez.

'Can we come? Maro and I? To Marabá?'

'It's a wicked place. The worst place outside Hell they call it. It wouldn't be safe.'

'Can I see the money?' asked Inez, and they laid out for her, on the dais of the holy statue, more wealth than she had ever seen in her life before. She touched each item reverently: the false passports, the travellers' cheques, the dollars held in a shiny clip, the floury gold-dust sifted out of La Senhora's flour. Enoque's wooden eyeball stared at the haul with wide-open lids. 'I don't think we'd better tell Mum and Dad. They'd use it to pull out,' said Inez. Then she added, 'The Baby really did good, eh?' And even La Senhora did not correct her grammar.

14

A CHANGE OF PLANS

It was a terrible thing, not to be able to tell their parents. Inez told Maro, and he said (as she had known he would), 'I could get a bike!' But then he too saw the need to keep secret the Find from Mr and Mrs da Souza. Apart from priests like Ignatius (who are supposed to reason on a grand scale) and those such as La Senhora and Valmir (who have no one to care for but themselves), grown-ups tend to think in terms of families and safety, of the future and how to ensure they survive to see it. It is not their fault. It comes with the job of grown-up. Maro and Inez were glad to know, in a way, that their parents would always be mother and father first, citizens second. But they also felt a sharp, painful shame at keeping their new-found wealth secret—as if they were hoarding it away just for themselves, denying their parents a chance to squander it. Inez realized that God knew all secrets; that God had put the Fixer's coat in the way of being found by The Baby, and very probably with a view to saving the town. But that only made it more odd: not telling Mum and Dad—as if they were not to be trusted with miraculous gifts from above.

Waking up, the morning after his sister told him the news, Maro remembered, with a sudden surge of excitement, about The Baby's Find. He wanted to leap out of bed and run downstairs and say, 'Isn't it fantastic? I'll get a Super BMX Kool Rider with dropped handlebars!' Then he remembered that he must say nothing, and the pleasure almost evaporated then and there. 'What when they find out?' he said aloud, knowing his sister would be awake and that she was a specialist in moral dilemmas.

'I don't know,' she said, to his surprise and disappointment. 'They'll think we cared less about them than the town. I don't think I can bear it.'

If Inez could not bear it, Maro was quite sure he could not. 'We'll tell them, then.'

'No. We won't tell them. We won't say we ever knew.'

'About the money?'

'About the money. About the plan to use it. About anything. Otherwise things would never get back between us the way they are now.'

'What, *lie*, you mean?' said Maro, rising up on one elbow and staring at her. 'Lie to Mum and Dad?'

Inez looked irritated and impatient. 'No. Just not mention it, that's all. Let Father Ignatius and Valmir take the blame. It's their plan. They're taking the money. They're the ones going to Marabá.'

'Maybe they'll run off with it and use false names and buy villas in Rio with swimming pools,' suggested Maro.

'Then they wouldn't have told *us*, would they? Besides, it's not *that* much money, I told you.'

Maro's head was resting against the wall just at that moment, and he felt a jolt to the woodwork below, which travelled up through the shingling and dislodged a chaga beetle close by his ear. He crushed the beetle, then looked out of the window. A *garimpeiro*, in a child's card-felt cowboy hat complete with peel-off sheriff's star, was swinging a pick against the foundations of the store, gouging out a hollow like the entrance to a badger's set. Maro pulled on the string which ran from his hammock, out through the window and in at Valmir's window to tug on the corner of his pillow. This simple alarm fetched Valmir's shotgun barrel out of the window over the storeroom, and his voice shouted: 'Private property! Off it, mister!'

The *garimp* looked up so that his toy hat fell back off his child-sized head. He bared the canines which were all that remained of his teeth, and spat a stream of coffee beans upwards in Valmir's direction. 'Who's gonna make me?' he asked, took out a revolver blackened all over with gun-oil, and fired it up at the window. He did it almost casually—as if the weapon were as much a toy as his hat.

Inez and Maro rolled out of their hammocks and pounded along the passageway to Valmir's room. They found him sitting amid a glittering kaleidoscope of glass fragments, holding his Manaus University T-shirt over the cut in his neck. The bullet had missed him, but the glass had not. There was a look of astonishment on his face, as if a western he had been watching had suddenly burst through the TV screen and gunned him down.

Even so, he showed great presence of mind. As Mrs da Souza came rushing up the stairs, her backless sandals flapping with a loud clap between each step, Valmir quickly instructed the children, 'Tell Ignatius I can't go with him. Tell him to take Honorio, instead. He'd do better than me, in any case.'

Raising her hands over her ears, as if to shut out her own noise, Mrs da Souza stood in the doorway and began to shout, like the landlady of some seedy boarding house cursing her tenants. 'This is the end!' she ranted. 'This does it! We're getting out of here! We're going. We're moving somewhere with human beings in it. Pigs! Animals! Beasts!' she bellowed at the broken window, while down below the *thud thud thud* of the pick undermining her house shook piece after piece of loose glass out of the window frame. Her arms closed around her children and drew them against her body so hard that they could feel her ribs through her cotton dress. 'This place isn't worth saving!' The words flew like bullets, out over Main Street, accusing the entire town of attempting to murder her family. That was when Inez and Maro knew for sure they dare not entrust her with the plan to save Serra Vazia.

Fortunately for Valmir, Honorio Furtado had seen the whole thing. It was fortunate, because when challenged, the *garimpeiro* with the revolver claimed to have fired in self-defence, afraid for his life at the hands of Valmir Zoderer. It was less fortunate for The Plot, because Honorio was needed as a witness by the local police. He dared not leave town for fear the student be charged with attempted murder.

Valmir commiserated with the priest next day, sitting up in bed, his neck bandaged to the width of his jaw, so that his head had the look of a coconut on a shy. It felt very similar. The children sat on his feet. 'You'll have to go on your own, 'Natius,' Valmir said. 'Or you could try Eleiser Juca. He'd be good. He'd know how to start a *fofoca*, surely, if anyone would?'

'I spoke to him,' said Ignatius and, ducking his head almost to his knees, he undid and re-tied his shoelaces with a care hinting at intense nervousness. 'He wanted paying to do the job. Five thousand. To set himself up again, he said.'

'*Five thousand cruzeiros?*'

'Dollars. You have to remember, he's lost everything.'

'He never had anything!' Valmir squealed in a voice constricted by the bandages.

'How do you feel?' asked the priest hastily, as if he did not want to continue the conversation.

Valmir considered how he felt. He felt as if he were sitting on top of a cliff while a flock of a thousand gulls pecked away the rockface below into more and more of an overhang. Any moment the cliff top would collapse into the sea below. 'Dizzy,' he said. 'Now I suppose Juca will want the money off you anyway, just to keep quiet about the phoney *fofoca*. It's finished, then. He's done for us, the selfish—'

'He doesn't know we've got any money. I was careful not to mention . . . ' Ignatius looked over his shoulder to both sides ' . . . The Baby's Find.'

'Where did he think you were going to get five thousand from, then?' gasped Valmir.

'Church funds. The church bank account. You know how some people are. They think every priest's got his fingers in the offertory.'

Maro piped up, 'Just like you said, Valmir. Isn't it, Valmir? That's what you used to say about priests.' His sister shushed him, but Maro had not been born a diplomat. 'Is there any?' he asked bluntly. 'Money in the Church funds?'

Ignatius's shoelaces were giving him great problems this morning. 'Hardly a bean. And what there is I can't get out. It's in the Bank Itau, you see. Hasn't opened its doors in months. I can't draw out a dime. At least I could tell Eleiser Juca that, hand-on-heart. Actually, I'm living on handouts from Senhora Ferretti, myself.'

'She could have left,' said Inez, suddenly, irrelevantly.

'Pardon, Inez?'

'I was just thinking. When she found The Baby's money, she could have taken it and left. Got out. She's always wanted to. She's got nothing to keep her here.'

They all considered this in solemn silence for a moment, none quite so solemnly as Inez, perhaps, since the others had never thought as badly of the schoolteacher as she had. 'I wish *she* could go to Marabá. Everyone in the world takes her word when she says something.'

But none of them could imagine La Senhora, in her blue dress and netted hair, striking gold with a pick-axe. Inez had to admit, she made an improbable *bamburrado*. But no more so than Ignatius with his angelic hair and clean habits and unfamiliarity with hard cash.

'The thing is,' Ignatius was saying, re-tying his shoelaces for a third time. 'What you don't know . . .' Valmir raised himself higher up the bed: he recognized bad news when he saw it coming. The priest looked at the children, as if to say that the news he had for Valmir was certified unsuitable for children below the age of sixteen. They did not take the hint. In fact they refused to go. 'The thing is that Alfredo Pessoa . . .'

Valmir looked blank. 'Who?'

'What's he done now?' asked Inez with a sigh. 'Last time I saw Alfredo he was waving a shotgun and pretending to be all kinds of a bandit. Mother says he'll never come to any good, that boy.'

'He won't get the chance now,' said Ignatius. 'That gun of his—it was cheap. Black market. Old, probably, and faulty. It went off while he was cleaning it—messing about with it, who knows? Someone found him this morning in the *barrancos*. Dead.'

'Dead.' The children repeated the word as if it was unfamiliar to them, incomprehensible.

'The police will want me to put in a showing. Then there's the funeral. Three, maybe four days soonest. Who's going to conduct it if I'm away in Marabá pretending to be a prospector? We'll just have to postpone . . .'

Valmir sank back among his pillows. So it was all off. Like wounded soldiers, whose worst fear is being shot a second time, all Valmir could think of was sitting in bed, helpless, when the floor collapsed beneath him and the house fell into the street. Serra Vazia was not intended to survive. Its fate was to fall into a hole in the ground. Otherwise Alfredo Pessoa would have chosen a different night to die, the *garimp* a different morning to shoot, someone other than Honorio to witness it. Sooner or later, hoping for the best had to give way to being realistic. He only had to look at the children's faces to see they had reached the same sad conclusion.

Downstairs, Senhora Ferretti stood beside the dining-room table in a small black straw hat of the kind people wear to church. 'She's dressed for Alfredo's funeral already,' thought Maro.

His mother said, 'La Senhora has very kindly offered to take you both to Manaus with her. Out of harm's way. We'll follow on in a little while, your father and I, when things have . . . settled themselves one way or another. And when Valmir is fit to travel.'

A bus had been summoned to Serra Vazia by a clutch of despairing townspeople who either could not bear to see their houses fall down or did not dare to be in them when it happened. They locked their front doors (even though gaps sagged round them big enough to let in a cat), left a note on the door in case distant relations called, then picked their way over the *barrancos* with all the worldly possessions they could carry, to where the Hole ended and the road began.

The bus driver was busy refusing permission for a plaster statue of a saint to ride on a bus seat alongside its owner without paying for the trip. La Senhora in turn bullied the driver. 'It's a disgrace. Charging full fare for children. Don't you know that in other countries . . . ?'

Mr and Mrs da Souza stood apart from those ready to board the bus. The storekeeper was blowing his nose in a handkerchief large enough to hide his tears; his wife stood tight-lipped, too angry for tears. That it should come to this! To entrust her children to another woman—and not even a relation! A strange groaning noise came from the fabric of the town—as if the buildings too were mourning the loss of their inhabitants. The bus started up, spewing filthy black exhaust fumes over those it was leaving behind. And Senhora Ferretti staked a claim to the back seat, so that the children could wave right up until the bus rounded the first bend in the road.

'I forgot my poster,' said Maro. 'My Manaus United poster. Behind my wardrobe door. I forgot it.'

'You can always buy another.' For a woman of great passions, Senhora Ferretti did not seem terribly moved by the loss of home and job, by the triumph of Greed over Civilization. She simply bounced her little cardboard suitcase on her lap and said, 'It's up to us now. The Father can't leave because of poor Alfredo. Valmir's been shot, and all the other men have some excuse or other to keep them home. So we shall have to do it ourselves, shan't we?'

Inez and Maro stared at her. 'Get off at Marabá, you mean? Pretend to be gold-miners?' breathed Maro in wonder and amazement. She snapped his mouth shut with one finger under his chin.

'Well, not *us*, naturally. But *garimpeiros* have wives and children, don't they? And when they've struck gold I presume they send those wives and children to town. "Go and buy yourself something nice, dear. Cash this gold in for me, while you're about it. Give the children a treat, dear."' When she said it, her face even resolved itself into the wrinkled mask of a seasoned *garimpeiro*.

'But the Baby's money . . .' Inez began to say.

La Senhora tapped her cardboard suitcase and then the side of her nose. 'All in here.' She seemed about to tap the top of her head, too, but she was only slipping the snood-net off the back of her head, loosing a coil of thick, glossy hair to sag down her back in restrained waves of greying brown. 'Are you on?' she asked with a sidelong flash of her samba-singer's eyes.

'We're on,' said Inez.

'On what?' asked her brother, bewildered.

'On our way!' said Inez.

15

BAMBURRADOS

La Senhora Ferretti emerged from behind the grey plastic curtains of the changing room like the sun from behind a cloud. She was wearing a yellow trouser suit dagged with black geometric signs and with little golden chains linking the diamanté buttons. A patent leather belt supported the hipster trousers against all odds, and a frilly polka-dotted blouse spilled out at cuffs and throat and between the join of jacket and trousers. Her sensible lattice-weave shoes dangled from one hand and she dropped them in the base of a tall pillar ash-tray. Inez was just thinking what a fine planter her mother could make of such an ash-tray. Maro went and looked at the discarded shoes. He had watched those shoes, it seemed, every day of his school life. They kept the shape of La Senhora's feet even when they were empty, and the heels were worn down like tree-stumps attacked by beaver.

'Not quite what I'd have chosen, given a free hand, but I thought perhaps a gold-miner's wife might have . . .' She stopped short of saying 'bad taste,' since there was nothing she hated worse than snobbery. 'A gold-miner's wife might . . . not have had access to cultured influences.' The streaks of blondeness in her hair, acquired at the hairdresser's that morning, chimed in with the yellow of her trouser suit. She chose a pair of gold sandals off the rack, but comfort demanded she change them for a pair of patent leather ankleboots. She had too much to do to waste time on limping.

Into the hairdresser's washhand basin and into the ear of every shop assistant who served her that day, she had poured the story of her husband's good fortune. 'Forty years of grubbing about and making do . . . then almost by accident really! . . . a lucky break . . . Stopped to water his *burro* and he could see it—there in the river!—plain enough to know it straight off. The Big Strike. The strike of a lifetime. The one he dreamed about all those years. Look at us!' she said. 'Yesterday we were hicks—no-hopers. Today we got it all . . . Go pick out a house, he said to me—for our old age, he said. Buy everything 'cept the car. Women can't be trusted to buy a car.' (They sympathized with her that she was not allowed to buy the car. If they were hoping for a large tip, La Senhora did not disappoint them.)

Maro and Inez looked on, increasingly hard put to recognize their schoolteacher. She picked up a hip flask in a street market and filled it with Coca Cola and would take large swigs from it in public places, smacking her lips as if it were hard liquor in the flask. When the children stood, frozen with terror, half-way across the race-track of Santa Anna Highway, La Senhora shrieked at them in a high-pitched, quacking voice: 'That's right. Get yourselves killed now, just when your father and I can afford to put you through school! Ungrateful brats! Typical!'

It was Proclamation of the Republic Day, and she bought them huge paper hats and giant hot dogs to eat in the street.

Father Ignatius had not been wrong about Marabá. If the Wicked and the Damned were to be allowed out of Hell once a year for a holiday, they would take it in Marabá. Its population seemed to be made up of gamblers, bandits, and men not quite honest enough to be either. Many were truck drivers between trips, spending their money as though they knew they would be dead next day. Perhaps the fortune-tellers in the little upstairs rooms with blue, neon signs in their windows always advised their customers: '*Spend it today, feller: last chance.*'

If the pavement was sufficiently empty of broken bottles, they fought each other. If there was no space for a fight, they spat on the litter instead. Swear words filled the air like *pium* flies at sunset—words so foul that once or twice La Senhora let her characterization slip for an instant, and put her hands over the children's ears. It seemed to be a town where no one had anything but loathing for each other. Only when they reached the hotel did the *bamburrados* of Serra Vazia discover that some people were more hated than others.

'Blacks to the back door,' said the doorman in royal blue uniform and gold braid—grand as an army general for all the seediness of the hotel.

'They're my sister-in-law's kids,' said Senhora Ferretti, and put her suitcase down on his feet.

The doorman picked up the suitcase and followed her through revolving glass doors held like great mirrors by brass claws and hinges. Dull lightbulbs glimmered all day in the lobby beyond. But while Maro and Inez hesitated outside, fearful that the circling doors would pulverize them like a food mixer, the doorman issued out again and bending at the waist shouted in their faces, 'Blacks to the back door, I said!' It was the first time in their lives they had ever been called by their colour.

'Why didn't you tell us about being black?' said Maro resentfully, when they finally found their way up the back stairs to La Senhora's suite on the top floor.

'I forgot you were,' said Senhora Ferretti, and that was that.

There was no point in trying to impress the other guests in the hotel, for they were already relatively rich—cardsharpers, drug dealers, coffee ranchers. Instead the three shared their 'secret' with every chambermaid, bell-boy, back-stairs porter, telephonist, and cleaner in the hotel. Behind the doors of the bedroom, La Senhora cleaned the cobwebs off the lamp and tuned the radio to some station playing classical music. In the lift, however, she turned up her own volume and spoke brashly of 'having a real good time now she had the goods'. They learned fast, Maro and

Inez—fast enough to strike off on their own, unaccompanied, and spread word of their father's gold strike.

The elevator doors in the nearby department store opened like the Gates of Paradise on an acre of glittering wonder. TV sets played computer games all by themselves, mini-Jeeps sped across the ceiling, suspended by wires, Shop dummies lounged and crouched and frolicked in everything from football shorts to evening dress, and a motorized Father Christmas rocked with recorded laughter in and out of a snowy grotto. 'I'll have one of those, maybe. My dad's just struck gold, you know. Serra Vazia? Where's that? No, up in the Nordeste. Place called Coaxi Ridge.' Pedal cars shone their headlamps and dolls spoke six phrases in American then wetted themselves. For ten minutes Maro and Inez played table football, and when the shop assistant told them to 'Give it a rest, you blacks,' they said their father had struck gold, and the shop assistant insisted they play for as long as they liked.

In the clothes department they kitted themselves out in shell suits and trainers big as plastercasts, nylon anoraks, and fluorescent shorts, knowing that anything other than poplin and rubber would rot in Serra Vazia's sodden heat. Perhaps that was *why* they did buy it—simply *because* in Serra Vazia it would have rotted.

At first they were simply playing—a delicious game. Inez would overact, pointing her nose in the air and demanding something from the topmost shelf. And they bought nothing, only implying that they might, wagging their wads of money to prove that they could. But soon their eyes began to adjust to the dazzle, and to focus on things that they had genuinely dreamed of owning—a dress with eleven layers of gauzy net beneath the topmost silk, a carbon-fibre fishing rod, a typewriter in a little carrying case, a strip just like the Brazilian World Team wore.

When at last they reached the power cycles, they came, by accident, to the brink of adulthood—there among the Vespas, the Lambrettas, the mopeds, and learner motor cycles. There the game stopped, and so did they. The lure was the lure of the Siren Singers for Odysseus, of the mongoose for the snake, of the magnet for iron, of the shore for the sea.

'I want it,' said Maro starkly, of the scarlet Kawasaki, and there was nothing to say in reply. 'Too dear.' 'Maybe one day.' 'Not us. Not our kind.' None of those answers applied any longer. The shop did not even seem to have any objection to the money of blacks, for there was a *negro*, even now, buying a Honda with a variety of credit cards.

'Too expensive,' said Inez. 'We'd use up too much of the money.' And yet she had sufficient money rolled up in the back of her knickers to pay for two, then and there. And all the other things they had played at wanting shrivelled into nothingness. The want was like a need. The pictures that came into her head—of herself riding the Kawasaki— were like a holy vision, a calling to own one. To own and ride it. To own.

'One between two, maybe?' said Maro, in the babyish whine of pent-up desire. But Inez had no vision in her head of a little brother riding pillion—only of herself, hair streaming, throttle roaring, leaning into the corner of Main Street and Lisboa Avenue. She would be someone else, signify something else. Life would see her coming, chrome and scarlet paintwork gleaming, and fall under her wheels before it had the chance to get away.

Maro was still arguing that *bamburrados* would never travel on foot, when Inez tugged an assistant by the sleeve and said, 'We want two of the Kawasaki KMX 125 trail bikes, please.'

'Don't we all,' said the assistant with a curl of the lip.

'Cash,' said Inez and, rummaging in her shell suit, brought out a wad of money. She relished the change it wrought in his face: as if she had turned from black to white in front of his very eyes. 'Our father's struck gold, you know. In the Nordeste. Near the Coaxi Ridge.'

'You want we deliver? All that way?' asked the assistant, alarmed.

And all at once Inez took fright at what she had done. Once she had stood astride Amilcar's big motor bike and kicked away the stand and felt the machine toppling over beneath her, too heavy to hold. She was the owner of a motor cycle now—and she did not even know how to take delivery of it. For all she knew, her house had already slid into a muddy hole and she was homeless, of no fixed address. 'Dad's still on the *barranco*. We haven't bought the new house yet. Give me all the bits of paper and I'll write you where to send the bikes.' The sales assistant did not see through her; he remained fawningly eager to serve. But Inez felt foolish, even so, as if she had been caught lying, impersonating one of her betters.

Back at the hotel, they told La Senhora about the motor bikes: they had to account for what had become of the money. 'It was our money to spend!' said Maro indignantly, trying to stave off a lecture. 'Sort of.'

But La Senhora said nothing. She did not inflate like a bullfrog and hurl censorious words at them as she would have done back in the classroom. She simply pulled on her new hat and adjusted the yellow veil. From behind the net came the comment, hardly spoken aloud, 'It's going to cost your father a great deal to put that store back in good order.'

Then the thought of those two scarlet motor cycles burned in Inez's head like the red hot coals of her iniquity, and she wished past wishing that she had never bought them, had never seen them, had never had to meet temptation face-to-face and find out how irresistible it really was.

In the afternoon, they all went together to the office of a gold-dealer, with The Baby's find of gold-dust and a bought map of the Nordeste. They had poured tea on the map, and folded it over and over again until the creases were splitting. They wrote here and there, in blue ballpoint, various disconnected words, as people do on maps. And there, where the Conspirators of Serra Vazia had decided upon for the Great Invented Gold Strike of Coaxi Ridge, they circled the pen's point round and round until it pierced the surface and bled ink into the strands of paper.

La Senhora bought a handbag with armadillo claws for clasps, and they went to the Town Hall and asked how to set about finding out who owned that particular piece of land on the Coaxi Ridge.

'Why d'ya wanna know?' asked the clerk rudely—a woman too bored to turn full-face towards them. 'How's it your business who it belongs to?'

'My dad found gold there!' said Maro. Inez slapped him round the ear. La Senhora hissed in his face. 'Quiet! Didn't I tell you to keep your trap shut?'

'He found gold?' said the woman, incredulous, sliding off her stool to peer at the map. 'Up *there*?'

'Ahahaha! Such an imagination. What? Gold? Aha aha! No,' said La Senhora. 'Of course not.'

'Of course not,' said Inez. 'My brother don't know what he's talking 'bout. He's simple, he is.' Maro cringed as though he expected to suffer physical violence once his female relations got him outside.

The clerk looked them over—this backwoods assortment of livestock dressed to the nines in expensive new clothes, and knew they were lying. It was a gold-strike, all right. A big one, too. She watched them hurry back out into the street, their query unanswered, then picked up the telephone and rang a friend as quickly as her fingers would pick out the numbers. 'Raoul? You're not going to believe this, Raoul . . .'

Outside in the street, the three bought palm-heart *empadas* from a street-seller, and congratulated one another on their acting, like seasoned old theatricals.

At the bank, they changed the foreign money into good Brazilian cash, and no one who was in the Bank Itau that day went home without mentioning 'the broad and the two black kids' who had brought business to a halt. First La Senhora had drunk the contents of a hip flask, then dropped some gold krugerands on the floor, then a handbag full of dollar bills and old beads, then a hat with a net veil. They were the kin of some *garimpeiro* who had struck a rich vein in the Nordeste *caatinga*.

Surely by now there was no one in all Marabá who did not know of the supposed strike. But still La Senhora racked her brain for ideas to get a *fofoca* up and running. 'What else?' she kept saying, as she paced the hotel room. 'What else should we have done?'

'If my dad really was a *bamburrado* . . .' said Maro, with half an eye on the TV.

'Yes?'

'If my dad . . .' He had had an idea when the sentence began, but as he tasted the words, his mind strayed down pathways paved with gold, to a fantasy where his father was really a miner who had struck gold. Money was coming in faster than water into a bath; new toys and possessions arrived by the truckload, and the calendar days turned over like the pages of a mail-order catalogue. On the TV, a selling programme was inviting viewers to phone in and order a digital watch with luminous hands and bleeping alarm. 'If my dad were really a *bamburrado*, I could pick up the phone and order that,' he said dreamily. La Senhora breathed out through her teeth—an extraordinary sound which woke Maro up out of his stupor. 'No, I mean, what I was going to say . . . If Dad had really just struck gold, he'd be sending for machinery now—digging and cutting gear, wouldn't he?'

'Now that's an excellent point!' exclaimed Senhora Ferretti. 'That really is a thoroughly good idea, Maro da Souza. Let's do it!'

Outside the doors of the Hotel Sublime, in front of the very eyes of the doorman, young children held up white sachets of crack and cocaine right under the chin of Senhora Ferretti— like bunches of lucky heather. 'Pretty lady buy a happy time?' they said in broken American, presuming her to be a foreigner. Inez winced for them, and waited for the blast of retribution to throw them on their backs in the gutter. But none came. La Senhora simply smiled at them and said, 'Not now, dears,' and went on her way. If only they knew, thought Inez, how narrowly they had escaped the wrath of La Senhora, terror of the school, glory of the monthly Musical Recital. There again, she was this woman, too, in the yellow trouser suit, and a samba singer with a jet black dress and disappointed ambitions for the Opera. Who *did* buy from the little boys and girls outside the Hotel Sublime? There was really no telling with people.

They took a taxi (taxi drivers spread gossip faster than anyone) and went to a massive hardware store on the edge of the city. It sold lawnmowers and Stihl power saws, and generators, and Massey Ferguson plant. 'Those men over there,' said Maro. 'They were outside the hotel when we left. Do you think they're following us?'

He thought he saw a frisson of fright shake La Senhora's veil, but it could only have been the breeze, for she said brusquely, 'I don't suppose so for a moment,' then summoned an assistant with a flourish of her armadillo handbag. They ordered a *chupadeira* to be sent poste restante to Coaxi Ridge. The sales assistant was every bit as intrigued as they had hoped he would be.

Outside they summoned a chequered taxi. But before it could nose its way across the flow of traffic, a black van accelerated out of the car-park and blocked its path.

'You want a lift somewhere, lady?' said the driver. It was one of the men Maro had spotted in the store.

La Senhora took each child by the hand and tried to walk round the rear of the van. It ran backwards with a screaming of tyres and a smell of hot rubber. 'Get in,' said the passenger, and there appeared, at the on-side window, what looked like a brown dog. It had large dilated nostrils and a lumpy, shineless head. In fact it was the barrel of a shotgun wrapped round in an old brown shirt. The collar points even looked like ears. 'Get in, I said.'

In fact, it proved impossible to squeeze all five of them into the front seat of the Transit van, and Maro and Inez were pushed through between the seats into the body of the vehicle. They lost their balance as it accelerated away. Fur hems caught them in the mouth. Beaded cuffs scratched them. Swaths and swags of cloth slithered off coat-hangers and smothered them as they tried to right themselves. What kind of people wore such clothes? Ostrich feathers and taffeta ruffles? The consignment swung in unison, with the movement of the van, grating their coat-hangers on tall, wheeled coat-racks, barging the children off their hands and knees and on to their noses.

'Hear you've had a bit of luck,' said the driver. He wore denims and a moustache like a bullrush balanced on his top lip. His teeth were apparently cemented together with gum; the whole van stank of spearmint.

'Do I know you?' asked Senhora Ferretti.

'Hear you struck gold up country,' said the passenger. He was indistinguishable from the driver except for a gingerish tinge to the bullrush moustache and one broken pane to his sunglasses.

La Senhora gave a hysterical whoop of laughter. 'Me?' she shrieked. 'Do I *look* like a gold-miner?!'

The van rounded a bend and rolled Maro and Inez through the forest of clothing. Little by little they crawled through the dense undergrowth until they found the rod-mechanism of the back-door lock and clung on. It was difficult to hear, from there, just what was being said.

'No. You look like a broad with too much money and too little sense to keep your mouth shut. Don't mess with us. You been sounding off all over about your old man's strike. Thing is, we could do with a break like that. We ain't had luck that good lately. We thought we might rub up 'gainst you—let some of it come off on us.'

'You seem to have jobs,' said La Senhora. 'Plenty don't.'

'Driving deliveries don't pay like what your husband earns.'

'What, when he's playing the pool halls, you mean? Oh, I don't . . .' There was a grunt of pain from the front seat which made Maro and Inez cling to one another.

'What are we going to do?' Inez heard herself whispering, knowing that she should be the one to be comforting her brother. 'It's all gone wrong!'

'No,' he said steadily. 'It's all worked out fine. We've started a *fofoca*, haven't we?' And she knew he was right. It was just that she had overlooked the dangers that might come from boasting of great wealth. La Senhora would have known all along the risks.

'She only has to give them the map,' said Maro. 'That's all they want. Then they'll let us go.' Inez nodded eagerly in agreement.

'You know what?' The schoolteacher's voice bellowed down the van. Perfect voice projection: they could hear every word when she wanted them to. What else would you expect from a singer? 'You know what you want?'

'Sure. We want that map you got in your bag. We wanna know where to go to get rich like you.' The contents of the armadillo handbag rattled on to the floor of the van. But there was no map.

'What you want,' persisted La Senhora, 'is a new business partner.'

'Where's the map, lady? Where's the goddamn map?'

'In the hotel safe, of course. As I was saying, what you and I both need is a change of management.'

'You get the map. We'll drive by there and you go in and you fetch it, lady. Or the kids get hurt.'

'*Yes, yes yes,*' said Inez to Maro. '*All she has to do is give them the map.*'

'Now that *would* be handy,' said La Senhora. 'They're

160

his, you know. My husband's kids. Well—do they look like mine?' and she cackled loudly. 'He's a pig. Always has been. A pig. What's a woman like me doing with a creep like him? A black. A *garimpeiro*.' She made them both sound like swear words. 'They take after him. It'd be worth it. It'd be worth it just to be rid of him and them. To cut it three ways.' She reduced both men to silence with her torrent of venom. 'You know what those kids did? Took six thousand outa my bag and bought themselves a couple of bikes—a couple of bikes. I ask you!' (She roared it over her shoulder.) 'That's why I keep it all in the hotel safe now. Kids. You got kids?' Clearly they had not. 'You'd pay to be rid of them, believe you me. You wish them furthest, every minute of the day. Yeah. OK. You drive by the hotel. I'll get you that map. On the way, let's you and I talk business.—Oh, and pull over here and dump the kids.'

'Dump them?' asked the driver querulously.

'Dump them. What you waiting for? Where's the problem? In the most dangerous town since Sodom? Two kids in expensive gear, running round the streets lost? They'll be picked off inside the day. Knifed. Beaten senseless. Dangerous woods, these, for rich babes, eh? No little birdies to cover them over with leaves and sing to them. There's hundreds living on the street, aren't there? What's two more?'

The van came to a halt. Maro peeped out and whispered, 'Traffic lights.' Then the back doors were wrenched open so suddenly that both he and Inez were toppled out on to the bonnet of the car behind. Its metal was hot and very thin. Inez remembered afterwards the look on the driver's face as two children were emptied out on to his car by the van driver in front who then jumped back behind the wheel and drove off without even missing the lights.

Louder than the traffic noise came a long roll of thunder. All day long it had been rumbling round the sky. Up in the forests it was already raining, people said. Now the rains had reached Marabá—the seasonal thunder which would

161

go on and on and on, stopping only like an old man's snores when he turns over in his sleep.

Maro and Inez stood on a traffic island amid a sea of traffic, and let the rain fall on them like cling film and seal over their eyes and mouth and ears and clenched fists.

'We've got to help her,' said Maro at last. 'She's in danger.'

'No. She wanted us out of it. You heard her. And like you said, she only has to give them the map.'

'She didn't mean it, then?' said Maro, and Inez saw that there were big tears standing in his eyes. 'About dumping us. About us buying those bikes.'

'Well, of *course* she didn't mean it, dummy! It was a ploy, wasn't it!'

'A what?'

'To get us out of harm's way! She was *acting*, wasn't she! She's been *acting* all round town, hasn't she?' She wanted to put her arms round him, but knew that then she would cry too and let La Senhora down. Someone had to keep their nerve. So she bullied him instead, and called him an idiot. She looked down the street for a sign of the black van, searching the lanes of traffic, the pavement and doorways and windows for a sight of La Senhora. But events and the city had swallowed up the van and its occupants, had eaten them down, closed around them like the petals of a giant water lily which shuts each sunset around its feast of flies.

'I want to go home,' said Maro.

'I think that's what she meant us to do,' said his sister.

'Well, maybe she did. But I wish she'd told us how to get there without getting knifed or beaten up or any of those other things,' said Maro with a sniff, shaking the rainwater off his nose.

'Well, so she did, you silly boy! Don't you ever listen?'

16

RAIN

'The bikes, of course! That's what she was telling us. Look where we are.'

They had been 'dumped', at La Senhora's suggestion, opposite the rear entrance to the department store. Inside it, their glorious red bikes stood propped on revolving stands of chrome and green felt, reflecting in their wing mirrors all the brash trash and glittering litter Maro and Inez had coveted so much.

'Ride home, you mean?' Maro was suddenly not so sure he could actually *ride* the bike that one day before had made his stomach ache with desire and his head spin with yearning.

'Before anyone comes after us for the sake of our clothes. That's what she meant. We look too well off to be safe round here.'

Maro agreed with that. The more he looked around him, the more he saw of Marabá's evils. The rain had washed the prosperous drivers and navvies and lumberjacks off the streets into the bars, leaving behind those too drunk to move, and those with nowhere better to go than the streaming alleyways, the dustbin fortresses. Rain bounced up off the pavements higher than a dog's eye, needling drug addicts, extinguishing the paltry cardboard fires of the homeless. The trash cans sang in orchestral unison under the beating raindrops. A dead cat raised a stiffened paw as a torrent of water shoved it down the gutter.

In the very doorway of the shop, a gang of street children sheltered from the rain, keeping look-out, like pirates through a sea fret, for likely victims. Their eyes lighted on Maro and Inez, and they stirred, like dreaming dogs, seeing not faces, only expensive, enviable clothes; not fellow children but fair game in a hunting season which never closed. Maro and Inez pelted through the traffic and along the side of the store towards the front doors. The street gang started after them, but they had no speed, no stamina in their undernourished, matchstick legs. Together they were a corporate clump of aggression; individually they were simply half-starved children.

Other street children moved among the men and women who had taken shelter from the rain in the big front porch of the store or who had just come out of the shop and hesitated now, peering this way and that in hope of a taxi. All the taxis were taken. So they clutched their pockets shut and watched the children with undisguised mistrust, like sheep infiltrated by wolves. Maro and Inez, too, clutched tight their pockets, though it felt almost as if they were cheating at this great game of Have and Have-Not. They felt they ought to be giving their fellow children an even break, letting them filch in turn from the gold filched by The Baby from a man who just as surely filched it himself from the gold-miners who had chanced upon it in another small-town shop doorway. Wealth was all a matter of seizing opportunities—usually out of someone else's pocket.

The assistant in the cycle department was startled to see them. 'Take the bikes with you? Now?' he said.

'I've got all the papers—the receipts and all that,' said Inez as confidently as she could. But she barely expected the man to believe her and agree to hand over two motor bikes. All she had ever given him was pieces of paper—some of them calling themselves cruzeiro notes, true, but paper none the less: sickly, tissuey paper slips similar to the ones Senhora Ferretti had pinned to Inez with hairgrips to represent flowers of the forest. A bike in exchange for paper.

A manager had to be sent for to unfasten the chains securing the bikes to their stand. He too checked the documents of sale, as if there must be some mistake. But though the rain hammered in protest against the windows, making mouths against the glass, the children were suddenly wheeling their scarlet bikes between frowzy dummies and glass showcases, between doll's houses and hobby horses. Inez stopped and bought a plush golden teddy bear for The Baby and stowed it in the pannier of her bike. Then she urged her brother on towards the lift.

The lift doors would not shut. They had to back out and bump the great bikes down the carpeted stairs. People stared at them as though they were Theseus and Ariadne leading a couple of Minotaurs out of the Labyrinth, tamed. True, the weight of his vehicle got the better of Maro and it crashed over on its side so many times that he began to cry silent concealed tears wiped away with a nylon cuff. Inez said nothing. The bikes were their only hope of getting out of Marabá and back to Serra Vazia where the rain was even now washing away time grain by grain, stone by stone, plank by shoring post. They had done all they could to start a gold-rush. Now they had to go back home and see if they had succeeded, see if the *garimps* would go.

Through the store they wheeled the trail bikes, through Haberdashery and Men's Clothing, through Luggage and Jewellery. Inez paused to buy two transparent plastic ponchos from the scarf department. Time and again assistants lurched towards them, floorwalkers flexed their muscles. But Inez had the paperwork: the words on the till receipt said that she and no one else owned the gleaming red bikes. She bent her head purposefully over the shiny handlebars and pushed steadfastly towards the door.

In the street doorway, the shoppers and street children looked on with open mouths, as if no one should be allowed to take such bikes out into the teeming rain, to wet the paintwork, to dampen the leather saddles. But Maro and Inez walked directly across the busy street and on to a garage forecourt where they asked a *caboclo* youth to fill the petrol tanks.

'Where's the petrol cap?' asked the *caboclo*.

Maro looked at his sister and saw that she did not know. Neither did he. 'That's for me to know and you to find out,' he snarled and the youth, accustomed to abuse from the good citizens of Marabá, searched the bikes until he found the shining screw caps.

'Keen bikes,' he said, thinking aloud.

'We just bought them,' said Inez and felt his envy splash up against her stronger than the rain.

'Wasted on the likes of you,' the boy's face seemed to say. 'Why not me?'

'We got lucky,' she said, by way of an apology, then she slipped her leg over the saddle and felt desperately for the kick-start.

'They've got key-ignition,' Maro told the garage attendant proudly, starting up his bike. Inez glared at him for not telling her earlier. As they rode down the high road, the street children ran after them throwing empty cans and whatever litter came to hand.

It was like being pelted with seed pearls and diamonds. The rain cut into their faces till they could not feel the touch of their fingers in wiping the water off their cheeks: felt only wet ice, not skin at all. The ponchos ballooned round then, filling up with wind, turning opaque with condensing sweat, though their faces gaped rigid, like frozen fish, and their hands felt fit to freeze to the throttles.

All the other drivers on the road were blind with rain, blinking windshield wipers, blearing through the clouds of steam rising off hot bonnets, blundering along the streets as if trusting to instinct. Wing mirrors bubbled with raindrops which obliterated all reflection. Trucks swung out of their lanes with the blart of a klaxon, and cars cursed back with shrill, tooting horns. Even the traffic swore in Marabá.

No sooner did they reach the edge of town and escape the terror of dense traffic, than the road diminished into slime-covered concrete. 'I ought to take you somewhere safe! A convent or something!' shouted Inez. But Maro called back that he could not hear, and increased his speed.

He looked so tiny perched up on the great throaty machine. He was too young for all this. She remembered, as if she were seeing someone else, how she used to boss and lecture her brother, tossing her head with sanctimonious certainty as she told him he would go to Hell one day for lying. What had they just been doing in Marabá but spreading a pack of lies, fostering one gigantic fib? What had she been thinking of, to buy him a machine beyond his strength and ability—because *she* wanted one, one of her own? Why had she not thought to buy him a helmet, some padding? What kind of a sister was she that she took so little care of her own brother? What kind of a daughter was she who, when entrusted with the welfare of a little brother, could not grow into the stature and wisdom of a mother? All the while she thought these thoughts, the figure of Maro, billowed about in grey polythene, grew smaller and smaller, until it seemed as tiny and fragile as a puppet. Then she realized that he was decreasing in size because he was increasing the distance between them, and she throttled up and raced after him, her back tyre chicaning through a puddle of mud.

The rain re-animated a whole dry summer's deposits of rubber from the road and spun it into treacherous swirls. The mud where tractors had crossed the highway, and the leaves torn down by high-sided trucks, were concocted into a deadly slurry by the driving wet, and in places a sheet of water lay across the road like a ford, and burst around them with a violent ripping noise.

It was a long, long way. The rain killed all sound—even the engine noise—reducing all five senses as surely as being asleep. A coma of rain. They rode on through it without knowing why they were doing it, unable to remember why they had ever left home. And without them noticing, the forest rose up again around them, sighing a three-thousand mile sigh of relief at the touch of the torrential rain. The trees bowed their heads; nothing else could humble them. Liana creepers coursing with water shivered like giant serpents. The earth crawled with water, steamed. The leaves steamed. The air turned to a green steam tasting, in a single instant, of a million sweet, rank perfumes.

Then the concrete road gave way to baked, compressed mud in the very act of reconstitution. The world was turning back into a swamp—the primordial mire before God separated water from dry land. Silver wraiths of rain moved between the trees, keeping pace, moving on the face of the fallen water. The tyre tracks they left behind them, beautifully paired, and patterned like the backs of crocodiles, slithered underground and disappeared from sight. The rain on their eyelids played tricks, in any case, smudging together what was there, what was not. Only the bikes were real: hot red dragons, panting, bounding, thirsting after the next petrol station and the next, carrying the children along towards some dragon lair in the forest.

Their bones felt pulled apart at the joints, their skeletons jangled and jarred into spillikins. The puny polythene ponchos burst and split and having split, rattled into tatters so that the red dragons were suddenly plumed, cockaded with white: something out of a carnival parade now, slewing and sliding and slithering drunkenly about. The children were no longer riding but wrestling with the bikes, willing and kicking them on, pitching their bodyweight over the wheelforks to try and make the tyres bite into the ground instead of skate across it. Daylight disintegrated into muddy darkness: their headlamps lit a yellow tunnel of rain, a glistening tongue of mud lolling out of the forest's mouth, waiting to lick them up. Inez began to cry despite herself, but the tears could not contend with the rain: they were outnumbered a million-to-one.

Maro was just then wondering, because his muscles hurt so much, whether he had died and gone to Hell. Inez had often told him he would—whenever he told a dirty joke or a lie. But he could not think how he had come to miss that *one particular instant* of dying. Had he not been paying attention? Inez was always telling him off for that, too. She and Senhora Ferretti.

What had become of La Senhora? What would he tell Enoque? That he had left her in the clutches of thugs, and scuttled away to safety? The old *garimp* would never speak to him again. 'Shoulda looked out better for a great lady like that.' And yet it seemed impossible that Enoque still existed: Enoque, or Serra Vazia or the rest of the peopled world. It must have been like this when God heaved down water in Noah's time, the moment before the tree-tops and the last sodden monkey and the last reaching hands of the swimmers disappeared underwater. All of them drowned, to clean up the Earth. Except that floods are not clean. They are muddy and miring. And people are not either good or bad, but a deadly jumble of both, so that you can't stop liking the ones people tell you are no good, and you can't lie back and take life easy even when you're one of the bad ones yourself.

Just as Maro thought these thoughts, a man-made shape loomed up in his headlamp, out of place among the chaos of Nature—a little conical roof on either side of the road— oh, and something joining them together . . .

Too late he realized the nature of the roadblock, and as he applied his brakes, the rear of the bike swung round, the tyre walls touched the mud, and the bike slid one way on its side, while Maro slid the other—under the HALT sign and on down the yellow beam of his own headlamp. 'Oh well. If I wasn't dead before . . .' he thought.

But the Earth had turned soft. Perhaps the whole planet was rotting like an old yam, turning brown. He picked himself up just as his sister stopped, dropped her bike and came running towards him. 'What did you think you were doing?' she shrilled at him. 'Look at you! Could've been killed! Are you blind or what? Why couldn't you look where you were going? Is that too much to ask?' Maro did not mind. Inez sounded like his mother, and just then he wanted his mother very much indeed.

The roadblock was the one outside Serra Vazia—where the armed police regulars sat all day to prevent strong drink from reaching the old Mount Vazia mines. The sentry boxes were deserted. Presumably the officers of the watch had decided no one of rank would be mad enough to venture out in the rain and find them derelict in their duty.

After that, Maro and Inez told themselves that the wet forest was familiar—that tree, that ditch—and drove very slowly, listening to the sick sound of over-oiled spark plugs, knowing that their machines were talking to them, but ignorant of the language. They rode knee-to-knee, slower and slower, until they began to wobble with the slowness and realize that they were actually afraid to reach Serra Vazia.

What would the rain have done to Main Street? To Lisboa Avenue? To the football field and the Church of Santa Barbara? What had it done to the excavations and the squatter shanty? To the graveyard? To the Serra Vazia Drugstore.

They forgot that the rubber factory chimney was down, and expected to see it, a warning of the town's closeness. So they arrived almost unaware, and found themselves in a lakeland setting: a landscape of meres and tarns and silence half rubbed out by the dense rain. They cruised across the football pitch, knew it must be the football pitch: the goal posts had long since been used to shore up some *barranco*, but the nets had been hung up in a tree for hammocks, and hung there still—even though there was not a living soul in sight.

The tents had gone. The latrines, filling with rain, had spilled their stinking contents out over the grass. Even the monkeys were silent now. They had jabbered and shrieked on the rooftops as they watched the *garimpeiros* pack up one by one. They had jibbered and screeched at the backs of departing pushers and gun-runners. They had laughed openly at the hurried departure of all those pretty dancing girls in their borrowed jungle feathers. And they had even scurried down to the ground and snatched mementoes from the Great Exodus, the columns of *garimpeiros* with their caravan of rusty machinery in tow. As they left, the outsiders were spat on by the first drops of rain.

But the monkeys had not followed them out of town. Unlike the *garimpeiros*, the monkeys had not harkened to the rumours of gold up in the arid Nordeste. There was nothing for monkeys in the *caatinga*: nothing for any breed of monkey. Only the human species of ape had to make the journey there in order to find that out.

Maro and Inez wheeled their bikes as far as they dared, on to what remained of the town square. Only oil lights glimmered in the windows of the houses, and there was no moon, only the occasional jag of lightning to reveal the change wrought on Main Street. The street had turned to water, the houses to arks afloat on a river. Every *barranco* was full to the brim, the planks washed away. It was almost beautiful. A Venetian scene by Canaletto. Candle-light on the water. But the new river flowing down Main Street bubbled, of course, as its water seeped inch by inch, further and further under the houses.

'They'd've had to go in any case, the miners,' said Maro. 'Maybe it was the rain drove them away, not us.' But they both knew that the miners would only have withdrawn, for the rainy season, to high ground, roosted nearby so as to be first back when the water subsided.

'No. The *fofoca* worked. We did it. La Senhora and us: we did it!'

They held hands, partly flummoxed by the lack of a safe route to the house, partly delaying the sweet moment when they would knock on the door (or scramble through a window) and triumph in their parents' amazement. '*We*

171

did it. We started the rumour. You should have seen us! *Bamburrados* for a day.' They simply stood there, savouring the thought, looking at the shabby sign down the road and on the other side:

SER-A -AZIA --UGSTO-E

The Bank Itau on the far side of the store clearly caught sight of them, too, and offered them the deference due to two returning heroes. For it curtsied. It spread its skirts of clinker planking and ducked down to the ground, losing its balance only at the last moment. The pitched roof slid off, like a drunkard's hat, and crossing the alleyway with extreme slowness, nudged the Store. No more than that: a corrugated roof jarring the mainframe of a timber house. But then the house was standing on rotten foundations eaten away by spade and pick and rain. It was all it needed to finish it.

The front wall fell entirely away and, for a moment, they saw into it, like a doll's house, a dark box divided into compartments by flimsy plasterboard and planking. There, all together in one room, around one table, one source of light, a little huddle of faces, black, blank, not even standing up, were the dolls of the house. Inez put out her hand as if she might pluck them out of danger.

But then the ground floor tilted and the table slid, and the lamp fell and presumably rolled into the flooded pit of the *barrancos*, for its light went out. Presumably the dolls, too, were spilled into the flooded street, for after the last sheet of corrugated iron fell, the last plank splashed down, the shabby sign, the window boxes, the panes of glass, the chimney stack, the bed, the shelves of stored baked beans; after these had subsided into the flooded trench, there was no noise but the noise of the rain hissing, hissing, hissing its contempt.

Maro wished God could have seen Noah's Ark go down like that—faulty design, perhaps, or holed by shipworm. Then He could have known how it felt to have no one of His own left in the World.

17

FLOOD

Parts of the house, in hitting the flooded street, floated and continued to spread apart, but in slow motion—not so much like an explosion as the gradual disintegration of the universe, planets slipping apart, rooms drifting in different directions. Though the drugstore's own glimmering light had been snuffed out, illumination in the street swelled a little, as other households opened doors and windows to look out at their neighbour's catastrophe. Torches shone across the oil-black floodwaters. Voices called out: 'Mr da Souza? Mrs da Souza?' But there was nothing they could do. They were trapped in their separate houseboats, sensing their own foundations melting, crumbling, swilling away.

'Find me a paddle! Something to paddle with!' said Inez. Maro turned to ask why and found her gone from beside him. She had leapt an immense strait of water to land with a splintering thud on a raft of overlapping planks. It was a piece of the store's front wall. The letters ERR VAS UG were overwashed by water as her weight sank the raft below the surface, but at least it stayed afloat.

Maro woke from what seemed like a long, paralysing coma, the thought of attempting a rescue driving from his head and heart and bowels the certainty that his parents were dead. On the contrary, he was suddenly sure they were alive, trapped beneath the water, holding their breath, waiting for him to do something. 'A paddle. A paddle.' He took up the words as if they alone could propel him through the water—but he could not find a paddle. Where was he supposed to find a paddle? What kind of a paddle?

Inez plucked one from the water—a piece of shelving ringed by the rusty rims of a dozen tins. She spread her weight across as wide an area as possible and braced herself against the impact of her brother leaping aboard. He covered the distance easily, fell across her, and would have plunged into the water beyond if she had not grabbed him by the seat of the pants. The refined machine cotton holding together his shell suit immediately gave way. With a ruff of tattered polythene round his throat and the back torn out of his trousers, he looked quite the clown.

Together they paddled the raft towards the spot where the store had once stood. Pots and cans and jugs and wooden kitchen utensils were still popping to the surface, like feeding fish rising. They collided with the living-room table, so heavy that it floated deep below the surface like a shipwreck's hulk drifting on the tide. The island of soil where the drugstore had perched, besieged by digging, was a black reef now, distinguishable from the water only by its lack of shine. One by one, floorboards were being removed, as gusts of wind raised swells of water to wash over the site. Disorientated by the continuous blinding, hissing, unremitting rain, by the dark and by terror, with five fathoms of water beneath her raft, Inez kept thinking herself back on the river, sweating beneath a paper dinosaur, pursued by phantom monsters. When a portion of the dark, shapeless but live, raised itself from the black quagmire of the house, she thought at once of the *Boiuna* and would have struck out at it with the paddle if it had been any closer.

'Here! Over here! Oh, *please*! For the love of God!'

'Dad? Daddy, is that you? Are you all right?'

He was not. He was hysterical—wild in a way that, for his children, pulled the pin out of the Earth's core and turned it into a live hand-grenade. 'It's your mother! She's trapped! Her legs! Help me! Why won't somebody help me? For God's sake help me!'

There was no sign of their mother. It crossed Inez's mind

174

that her father was wholly mad with grief. She had heard of that. She believed it. She could feel her own wits slipping away, the madness rising up all around like the flood.

They drove their paddles into the black mound where the living room floor had once lain, and ran the raft aground. A whole outcrop of earth fell away, crumbling into the Pit. When Inez stepped over the side, her feet sank into the ground, and vile slime closed over her shoes. As she tried to reach her father, she left behind her new trainers—one, two—sucked off by the mud. 'Stay here, Maro.'

'No!'

From the other side of the road, voices were shouting, 'Is someone alive over there? Da Souza? Zoderer? Are you alive?'

It was like a nightmare, running through molasses towards a goal which never comes any closer. At last, on the very furthest side of the island, on the brink of Lisboa Avenue's flooded *barrancos*, Inez reached her father. He was masked in black as if for the Day of the Dead, his eye-whites glaring, his legs and hands out of sight. He was something amphibious which had only half dragged itself out of the water. Only when she crouched down beside him could she see that his hands were raising above the level of the water a head, face-up, wearing a balaclava of black silt.

'It's her legs. They're trapped under something—a crate. It fell on her through the ceiling when the walls gave out. First the ceiling, then the stuff stored up above. Cigars it is. And cigarettes. In a tea chest.'

'Mam?' Inez could barely recognize her mother's face. Without its halo of dishevelled hair and gleaming with wet, unresponsive to the passionate kisses of the teeming rain, it had the look of the wimpled black madonna that stood in Santa Barbara church. And yet the eyes opened at the sound of Inez's voice, and the old familiar perplexed frown returned. 'I thought we got you away. Somewhere safe. I thought we did.'

'Just as well I came back,' said Inez, groping about for the crate. It must have been open, for all the while, cheap cigars—the ones her father smoked—kept popping to the surface. Like small fry chased by a catfish, they jumped a short way out of the water then fell back and floated away, their tobacco-leaf torpedo unrolling. 'If we can just empty the crate—make it lighter . . .' said Inez.

'Should've let you smoke, more, dear,' said Rosa da Souza to her husband calmly. 'One a day. It wasn't enough.'

Suddenly Maro broke surface having swum his way down the dug alleyway and into the Lisboa Avenue *barrancos*. The wash he created inadvertently swamped his mother and made her choke, and his father swore and circled her head with his forearms, fending off the water. He had the toes of his boots wedged into the side of the embankment, but he was sinking, little by little, as the plank shoring came adrift. And the weight of the crate was bearing down, too, compressing the muddy ledge Rosa was trapped on, pulling her under. Plunging their faces beneath the water, the children prised loose bundles of cigars, cartons of cigarettes, but the negligible weight made little difference. At last they discovered they were fighting not just the tea chest itself, but the ceiling joist which had fallen across it. It would have taken four men to shift that joist.

A length of bunting from the Independence Day decorations came drifting by. It might have been the very length of washline to which Valmir and Father Ignatius had pegged their poems. In their preoccupation with the digging, no one had bothered to take down the bunting. They had left it to bleach in the sun and lose its remaining colour to the rain. Now the storm had freed it, and the pennants floated by like flags of surrender, the washline snaking between them.

Inez grabbed the very last trailing end and brandished it incoherently in the air. 'Knots! Knots, Maro! I can't tie knots!'

He understood her more by intuition than what she said, and dived down again and tied the washline around the beam of wood. He came up coughing and gasping, begging for further instructions.

'We've got to get off to a distance and pull on it,' said his sister.

But the raft was gone. It had pulled free and drifted away. Inez bit her lip and seemed about to scream with the agony of frustration. 'Don't worry. I'll just have to swim,' said her brother.

'Hoi! You over there! Help's coming. What can I do? Is there anything I can do?' It was Father Ignatius.

Valmir Zoderer, swimming down the *barrancos* like a man pursued by piranhas, had shouted out loud as he swam. Bombarded with rubble from the falling house—a pane of glass, some jars of beef extract, a curtain rail with flowery cotton curtains, a metal chimneystack, he had kept on swimming—swimming and swimming, though he could have sworn he did not know how to swim. He had left behind him, to his perfect certainty, a dead man and woman and baby. By the time he reached the steps of Santa Barbara Church, and was pulled out by the priest and half a dozen others, the deaths had become his fault, the whole catastrophe of his making, the weight of guilt all his. He was convinced that he and his shotgun had failed to defend the da Souza's from the digging, from financial ruin, from the weather, and as a result, the da Souzas had died under the rubble of their home. The wound in his neck had re-opened and he was rigid with shock.

So the priest and the other men had piled their coats over him and Ignatius had set off back down Main Street, climbing from house-front to house-front, wading and swimming and clambering along to the Town Square where there was sufficient dry land left to stand on and call, 'It's Ignatius! Is there anything I can do?'

177

'*No! No! No! No! No!*' da Souza screamed, back across the water, recognizing the priest's voice, thinking he was offering the Last Rites for a dying wife. 'She's not dead! We're going to get her out! The kids and I, we're going to get her out! Go away! Go away! *Go away!*'

'Hush, Dad . . . Father Ignatius?'

Was that a girl's voice? Ignatius shone his torch, and it strobed briefly over a slimy, shapeless mermaid. 'Inez, is that you?' Unbelievably, the next moment, he saw Maro da Souza swimming towards him across the flooded street, with a piece of rope between his teeth, trailing a length of bunting behind him like some foundering cruise-ship. He always could swim like a fish, that boy. Always.

Maro thrust the rope at him, and Ignatius took it in his own teeth while he pulled the boy out. Like a gaffed fish Maro lay along the ground for want of breath. 'Pull on the rope! Pull on it!' he gasped.

But it was ridiculous, futile. For one man and a boy, by pulling on a washline, to exert any force worth a mention.

'Maro! The bikes! Fetch one of the bikes!' Inez called again out of the darkness.

Bikes? Ignatius looked around him, bewildered. The rain hissed his stupidity. It filled his eye sockets with a blindness like old Enoque's. What bikes? Pushbikes?

Had they not been red, those shiny heaps of metal, lying on their sides, still steaming at the ribcage, even Maro would never have found them again in the dark and the downpour. It was not until he tried to lift one, to rest it back on its tyres, that he found out how exhausted he was. Ignatius was no better—worn out by just the effort of reaching the town square.

But somehow, between them, they righted one bike and wheeled it to the brink of the water, tied the washline to the frame under the saddle, and started up the motor. Maro climbed aboard—'Do you know what you're doing? No, boy! Not that way!'—He let out the throttle and shot away towards the dead lightbulbs and closed doorway of

Tony's Disco, with Ignatius yelling after him, 'No! Not that way! Not like that! *That's no good*!'

The rope and its bunting paid out to its limit. The jolt of reaching the rope's end threw the bike five metres in the air. Maro came off over the handlebars, seeing first the sky, then the ground, then the wall of Tony's Disco. He landed on the mountain of discarded cardboard boxes and polythene, the flotsam from a sea of Coca Cola. The bike's engine screamed and, across the water, in an eerie echo, came an answering scream.

Mrs da Souza, freed for an instant, had then been crushed again as the rope went slack and the beam settled back into place. Her scream was cut short, for as the weight bore down on her again, her face was finally dragged below the surface and out of anyone's reach.

Father Ignatius picked up the bike. Miraculously, the engine was still throbbing. He got on, let out the throttle, scuffing his toes gently, gently along the ground to keep his balance. It was years since he had straddled a motor cycle. When the rope was all paid out, he took up the strain, then leaned right forward over the wheel-forks, his nose almost on the mudguard, to keep the front wheel from lifting. He revved and he revved and he revved, and the little engine whined and squealed and smoked like a thing tormented.

'Pull, you bastard! Pull!' he shouted at it, and its headlamps lit up his streaming face contoured with throbbing blood vessels. His yellow hair hung down from his skull and wiped dirt off the mudguard. 'Move, you red pig! It's why you came here, isn't it? So shift yourself, God damn you!'

With a belch of black smoke, all the oil burned off the red-hot engine block and it seized solid, with a noise like a wing-eared *chonchon* closing on a man's soul. He shut on the brakes with both fists, but the bike still skidded backwards, pulled by the weight of the heavy wooden joist settling back into place. Ignatius slid off the bike and fell on his knees in the wet, covering his face with his hands. He had failed.

179

'*We got her! We got her!*' Inez's little voice flew down the flooded street like Noah's dove, triumphant. The weight had been lifted for just long enough to pull Mrs da Souza from under both crate and beam. She had been underwater for just half a minute. Now she was out, safe, saved. She breathed the air as if it were a treasure to be excavated out of the rainy sky.

The other men who had helped Valmir, had finally tracked down a rowing boat and, though it had no oars, were paddling it with their hands across to where the neighbours lay stranded. They made a stretcher out of a broom, a piece of bannister and a coat. 'There there, Mrs da Souza. Soon have you in the warm.'

As they gently lifted her into the boat she asked, 'Where's my baby?' The men looked at one another and said nothing. What was there to say, after all?

Then the rain suddenly stopped. Just like that. As if it had caught its breath in one convulsive sob. Tears dripped off the eaves of the houses left standing. For the first time, it was possible fully to open the eyes and to see the altered shape of the street: the yawning gap where once a store had stood, once a bank. What an intolerable loss—for a town to lose its store. For a family to lose its baby.

Meanwhile, Valmir Zoderer, stirring beneath a heap of coats on the floor of Santa Barbara Church, looked up to see the madonna and Saint Barbara herself looking down at him with raised eyebrows and expectant smiles. Their wooden cheeks were spotted with excitement—or was it embarrassment at the presence of this unbeliever in their midst, this deserter of his friends, this failed writer, this despicable fool wetting their floor like a stray dog? The carved baby nestled in Mary's arms looked down at him quizzically, wondering what he would do now, what he was good for.

Throwing off the coats, Valmir got up and went outside again on to the steps. The cold slapped him in the face, as he was sure the madonna would have liked to do. He stepped off the porch and, sinking up to his chin in water, began the long swim back towards the family he had deserted. He could not think what good it would do; he only knew he should not have come away. The da Souzas were his family, as much as his own natural parents. He could not just lie on a church floor doing nothing. He would help to find their bodies, at least.

Just in front of the burned-out hulk of the Hotel d'Ouro, where his feet could touch down on the rubble from the fallen building, the rain stopped all of a sudden. Just like that. The silence made his ears sing. He blinked to squeeze the last raindrops off his lashes. Floating towards him, he saw what looked like a hip-bath or a sink—white and shiny. He put out his hands to stop it drifting into his face, and found it was not enamel but wood, gloss-painted wood.

Beneath the water his toes collided with the hotel safe—the one that had caused such a furore the day after the fire. He stepped up on to its open steel door, and was able to see over the rim of the cradle. There, having slept through the end of one world and the beginning of the next and still sleeping, lay The Baby under a white wool blanket with lambs on it. Lambs and bluebirds and doves.

18

PEPITA

They looked like a low-budget Nativity tableau, sitting about a cradle, with towels draped over their heads and blankets wrapped round them. There was a poverty of animals—no donkey or oxen—but in the rear of the bus garage inspection sheds a wheel-less bus and a red motor cycle seemed more appropriate anyway. One small ferret-like creature rooted about among the tangle of brake cables in preference to worshipping at the crib.

'We almost weren't here when you got back,' said Enoque Furtado, covering one eye to look round for his pet. 'There was word of a big strike up in the Nordeste. Well, that's where everyone's gone. We'da gone, maybe, but I wasn't fit yet. Everyone else went. Everyone else cleared off up there. On the *caatinga*, of all places! Imagine.'

'But, Enoque, don't you see? That was *our* gold strike,' said Inez. 'The one we planned together. The phoney *fofoca*. To make all the *garimps* move on.'

Enoque looked doubtful. 'The Indians knew to get out anyhow. They knew the Forest Spirits were about at the end of their tether. Did you hear there was a *Boiuna* seen?'

'But, Enoque!' Maro protested. 'It was you helped us fix it for the Indians to think that! It was you suggested it!'

Enoque looked more dubious than ever, and mistakenly covered the wrong eye so that he lost sight of them altogether. Things which happened at a distance—in the spirit world or in the Nordeste, or in the imagination, or in the past were all equally credible to him who believed everything people told him. Besides, his mind was only half given over to the question of gold and the exodus from the town. He was also thinking about the schoolteacher lady, the one who had nursed him. She had not come home with the children, and that was sad. He wanted to talk about her—had tried to ask questions—but his young friend Maro was oddly unwilling to say what had become of La Senhora. Enoque hoped she had not come to any harm. ''Cos I'd lay down my life for a lady like that,' he said absently, and his brother patted him on the shoulder gently, knowing his thoughts and feelings.

'So where did all this money come from to splash about in Marabá?' said Mr da Souza to his children. 'Where did you get it?'

Maro and Inez stared at their feet. This was no Christmas tableau after all. Father and mother were just about to find out the full extent of their children's deceitfulness and treachery. It was time to admit that they had kept their secret to themselves, not trusting their own parents sufficiently to confide in them. There would never be a Christmas again. Not really. Not with that kind of hole driven through the heart of the family.

'It was found. Senhora Ferretti found it,' said Father Ignatius, all of a sudden. 'After the fire. She told me. We thought it was the best use for it.'

'I could think of one or two other things to do with it,' said Mr da Souza bitterly. His elation at finding himself and his family alive was starting to crumble as he took stock of what was lost. His shop was gone, his house and livelihood. The town that remained standing was barely habitable. The rainy season ahead would pull down the rest of the houses one by one into the abandoned *barrancos*. He was prepared to thank God over and over. He would do that till his life's end. But he was hardly ready to thank the priest and La Senhora for squandering a windfall. He was hardly ready to congratulate his children for coming home on gleaming motor bikes when his every possession was floating about in the Pit outside.

'I'm sorry we didn't have time to consult anyone else,' said Ignatius heavily. 'I suppose she told you children about the money when you were on the bus, did she?'

How well he lied! Inez was so much in admiration of his lying that she forgot to answer.

Not Maro. 'Yes! She told us she'd got the money after we got on the bus, yes,' he said, keeping scrupulously to the facts, proud of skirting so agilely around the truth. But it troubled Inez, that Ignatius could lie with such conviction, even though it was for her sake. First La Senhora, now the Father. All the simple rules for life were falling apart. 'She told us we had to spend the money as if we were rich,' Maro was saying. 'So we had to, didn't we? Had to.' It was his excuse for owning the bike. 'She said we had to make a stir—make people notice. You should've seen the way people looked at us on those bikes, too! They'd've killed us to get their hands on them, truly!'

A desolate gulf opened up in Inez as deep as the mine workings outside. 'But we didn't have to buy the bikes,' she said. 'We didn't. We could've just made like we were going to. Could've talked about it. We didn't have to go ahead and do it.'

'Then you would never have got back here in time to save my life.' They had all thought Mrs da Souza was asleep, tucked up on a pair of old bench seats unbolted from the bus. Her leg was broken and Eleiser Juca had volunteered to ride to the nearest medical post for a doctor. That is why only one bike stood in the rear of the shed, its engine shot.

'We'll sell them now though, Mum. We'll sell them and give Dad the money.'

Mrs da Souza adjusted her position awkwardly, painfully and said, 'No. God wanted you to have those bikes . . . And if He didn't, I do. God knows, there's nothing else we can give you children for an inheritance.' She was not talking from the depths of despair. Her face, now that the mud had been washed off, was not crossed through with lines of worry. The worry had been always to keep going, to keep the store going, the house vertical, to manage, however bad things got, and just hope they got no worse. Now that everything had gone, she was almost relieved. She had let go of all that leaden anxiety and was floating, consequently, in mid-air. 'Do you hear that, Eduardo? I want them to keep their bikes.'

'There's only one now,' said Maro forlornly. 'There's only Inez's one. The other's bust.'

'We can share,' said Inez.

'*Really? Truly?*'

'Of course.' It would be a relief not to be the only one with such a valuable possession.

'At least the mining's over,' said Mr da Souza. He had his fingers entwined in his wife's hair, and it was as if some of her peacefulness was conducted through the damp strands. 'At least that nightmare's behind us.'

'We must be grateful to Senhora Ferretti for that,' said Father Ignatius, and there was a reverential silence, as when the dead are honoured in their absence. 'That's why I believe we ought to imitate her . . . her *spirit of enterprise*.'

The peculiar blue light from the paraffin heater cast an uncharacteristic villainy over his angelic features, and turned his yellow hair slightly green. He took on an amphibious look which somehow befitted a town half sunk in mud. 'I believe she interpreted our . . . lucky find as God's way of . . . how should I put it? Taking a hand.'

They agreed one by one, some more grudgingly than others.

'So that if we pursue that reasoning further, we might say the events of tonight were somehow *meant*. Intended.' There were fewer murmurs of assent. It was difficult to see how ruin and homelessness contributed to a Divine Plan for Good and Happiness. ' . . . because the store wasn't the only place that fell apart this evening,' said Ignatius. 'And I've always thought *initiative* was the most useful of God's gifts.' Then, withdrawing his hands inside his sleeves and addressing his good wishes to Mrs da Souza, he left—

185

rather abruptly, they thought, for it was hard to see what pressing business he could have at two in the morning.

'What did he mean, "not the only place"?' said Mr da Souza. Understandably, as his house fell down round his ears, he had not been in any position to see what other catastrophe was befalling the street.

'Well the bank went too, of course,' said Maro prosaically. 'It was the bank knocked down our place.'

'The bank?'

There was a pause in which the smell of the distant river and its rotting vegetation mingled with that of the giant lilies digesting flies, the anaconda chewing on a fat rat, the dead swimming from their graves. It was the bottom of the night, and just once in the history of Time, it seemed as if the night halted and they had the choice—that huddle of mudlarks in the back of the bus shed—whether to stay there for ever or pull themselves up into the brightness of the following day.

Without a word, they got up. Towels and blankets fell to the floor and thirstily drank up oil stains. Even Mrs da Souza raised herself on her elbows and nodded at her husband, as the able-bodied moved outside into the lesser darkness of the night-time street. 'For everyone, mind!' she called after them. 'It must be for the good of the whole town!'

They stood on the edge of the *barrancos* and looked out towards the gap where the Bank Itau had stood the previous day—repository of Mr da Souza's savings, of the church funds, of various union monies and local party funds, mining company accounts, and all the other deposits the townspeople of Vazia had despaired of seeing again, after the bank closed its doors and the staff became gold-miners. There had never been a fortune inside there, of course. An impoverished town supports impoverished banks. Already the bank notes left loose behind the counter grilles were floating profitlessly on the dirty floodwater. But there were coins, too, and bound wads of notes too heavy to float, bundles too securely locked away for the mud crabs to have reached them, safe doors that had even kept out the water when the Bank Itau subsided into Main Street. There were also cold hammers and jemmies left behind by the *garimps*, an acetylene torch from the bus station.

And three hours of night left in which to strip the bank of every remaining centavo.

When, at the end of the rainy season, the bank's city administrators arrived in an armoured truck to assess the insurance claim on their Serra Vazia branch, they thought at first they must have come to the wrong town. For they had heard Vazia was a shambles—a hole in the ground overhung by houses, a string of *barrancos* swallowing up the buildings one by one. What they found was delapidated, true, and there was no denying that the Bank Itau had gone. 'The *garimpeiros*, you know,' a passer-by told them, as they scoured the town for it. 'They came down on this place like a plague of locusts.' He directed them to the site where the bank had once reputedly stood, but though the administrators searched, they could find not one brick, one rail, one pane of glass, one cotton coin-bag to prove it had ever existed. In front and behind the bare, level site, lay a street so smooth that hardly a puddle formed when it rained. Vazia's notorious Hole was missing, too. From the freshly scrubbed steps of the Santa Barbara Church, right up to the town square and its new public colour television, ran a new, float-concrete road. It still bore the pattern of the smoothing boards. It also bore clusters of initials here and there, and the footprints of some small, ferret-like creature which must have crossed, while the concrete was still wet, between the bakery and the Serra Vazia Drugstore.

They asked at the drugstore, of course, what had become of their bank. The storekeeper offered them each a cigar and a cup of coffee, but little in the way of solid information. And the coffee was spoiled by the strong smell of fresh paint and newly oiled floorboards. The rest of the townspeople were no more forthcoming—from the taciturn Indians in the shanties, to the pair of transients camped in an old trailer beside the newly seeded football pitch. 'Some of these upriver folk: they're like a different breed. Dumb animals,' said the insurance assessor, writing off the contents of the Vazia Branch Bank Itau as an affordable loss.

On the way out of town, they passed, coming the opposite way, a large black Transit van driven by a matronly lady in a yellow hat and veil, singing samba songs at the top of her voice. It confirmed them in their opinion that the backwoods were riddled with villains and birdbrains.

'But how did you get away from those hoods?' demanded Maro. 'Did they just let you go when you gave them the map? We thought for sure they'd murder you once they had it!'

Inez rapped him sharply over the top of the head. 'Of course we didn't think that. We'd never have come away and left you there alone with them if we'd thought that. I *told* you she'd be all right, Maro, if she just gave them the map . . . But you were gone an awful long time, Senhora,' she added. She could remember how worry had given way to the most dreadful foreboding as, week by week, the winter elapsed without news from Marabá.

'"Awfully", Inez, not "awful". It's adverbial, you know. But yes, I'm sorry I couldn't get back here before. The roads were quite impassable after those first rains—for a vehicle like mine, you understand. And I had to go to Manaus, too, of course.' She sat like a queenly monument, on a large, derelict armchair. Someone had balanced it on top of the ice-cream freezer outside Orlando's Juice Bar, so that she overlooked the town square and the host of faces assembled to welcome her home. There was not a soul left in town who did not know how La Senhora and the da Souza children had created a *fofoca* and saved the town from the Gold Rush of '93. The vague myth had grown up of her giving her life in the cause; so that by the time she arrived back—contrary to anyone's expectations—it was almost like a visitation by one of the holy martyred saints.

'I didn't *give* them the map anyway, my dear Inez,' she said sternly. 'That would hardly have been in character with a greedy woman prepared to betray husband and children. No, certainly not. I *sold* them the map. "You give me this van," I said, "and the map's yours. How you settle the matter with my husband when you get to Coaxi is entirely up to you and that gun of yours."'

In recounting it, she relived it, her grandest *coup de théâtre*, her career's most crucial role. A patter of applause ran through the crowd—even among those who had not heard tell of the thugs before.

'So! Now you have a van, lady!' exclaimed Enoque, his hat clasped to his breast, his upturned face shining with admiration.

'The town does. The town,' she corrected him.

'And something really worth selling inside, I hope.'

'Theatrical costumes!' declared La Senhora with a broad, theatrical grin. 'Theatrical costumes for the Opera House in Manaus. I delivered them myself. I must admit, it gave me a certain amount of . . . satisfaction. Cash on delivery.'

The crowd groaned with pleasure. How fitting that their town diva should have profited after all from the Halls of Fame. How apt that, even now, the thugs who had thought to buy cheap the route-map to a secret cache of gold were digging up cacti in the dusty *caatinga* at the end of a wasted journey.

Later, in private, Senhora Ferretti put on less of a show. She admitted, though only to her closest friends, to feeling very slightly bereft. 'I told so many people about him. I quite came to believe in him, that husband of mine. Digging away in the Nordeste, waiting for his children and me to come back . . . I even thought I knew how he looked, you know? He smoked a pipe, and wore blue denim bib overalls and liked to drink herbal tea out of the saucer. And what with the gold strike, his hair had grown really rather unkempt so that . . . What a silly old woman I must have become.'

She broke off, lowering her head so as to hide her face from ridicule. But before even Ignatius could find the correct, tactful response, she had snapped open her armadillo handbag and found there a new fund of words. 'I brought back the proceeds, of course—but you seem not to need them quite as pressingly as I imagined. I really am most impressed with how you've put the town to rights.'

'You keep the money,' said Mrs da Souza quietly and, as she brought round the herb tea to her guests (on a pretty silver salver made from a wheel hubcap) she pinched shut the clasp of La Senhora's handbag again. 'You'll need something for your retirement if you're going to stay on at the school. Teachers are paid so very badly, I always think. You are staying, I hope?'

'I hardly think the likes of Inez and Maro would prosper in this world without benefit of a sound education,' said the schoolmistress, scowling over her glasses at them in a way that still had the power to curdle their blood.

'I'm glad,' said Mrs da Souza. 'Because Mr da Souza and I were wondering if you would stand godmother at the christening.'

'*You're going to christen The Baby?*' Father Ignatius slopped his tea into his lap and did not even dab at the stain on his jeans. Mrs da Souza reproached him with a crushing look.

'We thought Pepita would be a good name,' Mr da Souza added. 'Since she kept turning up in the *barrancos*. Pepita. "Little nugget." I hope you all approve.' He rocked the cradle absently with one hand, even though The Baby was not in it.

So Pepita was christened: not because her future held out any greater hope of security than it had done before, but because what there was had come to seem so much more of an inheritance. Serra Vazia would always be hard put to survive, born during a boom-time long past, too isolated to be of interest to government or economy, its population dwindling, its streets empty of gold. But though it looked much as it had done before the gold strike, there was something different—intangible—blowing down Main Street and Lisboa Avenue, mustering in the evening air even before the *pium* flies could do so.

Perhaps because of his injury, Valmir Zoderer was slowest to sense the air of renewal. 'I'll never write again,' he remarked, seeing Father Ignatius peg up a poem entitled 'Pepita' among the other string literature in the town square.

'Whyever not?' asked the priest sharply.

'Guilt, I suppose. Call it my penance. Look what I achieved. I used to write letters for the Indians and the *paisanos*, they never did any good. I wrote to the Press: they made a laughing stock of the town. I wrote to the Government—they sent in the troops to fleece us. I'll never put pen to paper again. It was *doing* saved this town. It was someone ready to get up and *do* something. I think that's what I'd better try. Get a job. Go to the city. Do something constructive instead of messing about pretending to be a writer—pretending that writing can change anything.'

'Have you ever thought of fiction?'

'What? Making up stories?'

'Well, as I see it,' said the priest, apparently still more

interested in reading the various shreds of verse and love poetry strung up beneath the TV, 'you could equally say it was Fiction that saved the town. An invention. Put about by word of mouth, nothing else. Just words. Amazing that words could do what shotguns and lawyers couldn't.'

'Yes, but *fiction, blagh*. I wanted to write about truth and justice and Man's inhumanity to Man. God's goodness and so on.'

'God's g— Goodness!' said Ignatius to himself. He turned his head away so that Valmir should not see the grin, but finding he could not wipe it off, pulled the neck of his Papal Visit T-shirt up over the lower half of his face. It rather startled and confused Valmir. It was in a slightly muffled voice that Ignatius said, 'Why? Do you think fiction has nothing to do with Real Life? Suppose you read in a story about what happened here. Would you really suppose none of it had ever happened?'

In unconscious imitation of his friend, Valmir Zoderer plucked the neck of his T-shirt up into his mouth and held it between his teeth, rapt in thought. 'Write about what happened here? As a story, you mean?'

And Ignatius knew (even though Valmir did not) that the words were already being mustered, the sentences recruited, the paragraphs conscripted, the chapters deployed like troops on a battlefield. He said goodbye, but Valmir was too lost in thought even to notice him going.

Ignatius walked slowly back down Main Street, enjoying the freshness which comes to a river town after the rainy season is over. Mr da Souza was smoking a cigar on the boardwalk outside the new store. They waved to one another. Further out, up the hill, a red motor bike leaned against the wall of the schoolhouse—a peculiarly grand status symbol, somehow, for a class of barefoot children to glory in. He could hear the ringing tones of La Senhora teaching Portuguese history:

'... *Henry the Navigator—that greatest of all explorers, to whom the Portuguese-speaking world is so deeply endebted . . .*' What a voice! He resolved to call for a samba by way of an encore at the next monthly Recital in the church. But he tended to disagree about Henry the Navigator. He could think of more useful things than exploring the world. The World was rich in such singularly unpleasant places and practices. And he could not help smiling at the recollection of Senhora Ferretti's latest holy confession.

She had admitted to 'keeping back' certain of the costumes she had found before delivering the van's consignment to Manaus Opera House. Her old blue dress would simply stand no further repairing, she explained, without making excuses, and the yellow trouser suit seemed 'inappropriate' for a woman in the teaching profession. He had nodded soberly and told her to give away the trouser suit and the hat with the yellow veil to someone in need of cheering up. He wished he could have congratulated rather than admonished her. But theft was theft. He wished even more that he could tell someone else the secret of the costumes, but of course the sanctity of the confessional made that impossible. Still, he rather sup posed it might leak out of its own accord . . .

Both Maro and Inez pretended to read the absorbing facts in their books concerning Henry the Navigator (1394–1460). But Maro's eyes were really turned towards the window and the gleaming handlebars and wing mirror of the Kawasaki just visible above the sill. He had plans for him and his sister to become despatch riders after leaving school—racing between the villages and towns of the Amazon, building up such a reputation for speed and daring that they would own a fleet of bikes one day and bring work and fabulous wealth back to Serra Vazia.

And Inez was watching La Senhora, through the lashes of her top lids, studying the amazing dress with its ruched waist and cross-over bodice. Green satin was not a common sight in Serra Vazia. Though the hand-turned hem stopped at mid-calf, Inez had the impression that it should not have done—that it had once gone on, swagging downwards into a train, or fluting outwards into a dado of the same grey fur as trimmed the cuffs. Yesterday's dress had been red brocade, fastened with golden buttons. If there were more dresses like this in store, life in the classroom of Serra Vazia was never going to be quite the same again.

But there was only one other garment, and that La Senhora was saving for her monthly concert in the church. She had only put it on once so far, in a photographer's studio in Manaus. It was a costume originally intended for Cio-Cio-San to wear in *Madame Butterfly*—a floor-sweeping kimono woven with moth-motifs and fastened by a broad obi of midnight blue shot-silk. Perhaps she would not even dare to wear such an extravagant piece of theatrical nonsense in front of her friends and neighbours and pupils. She pondered this intermittently, between bursts of rhetoric in praise of Henry the Navigator.

Even as she did so, the photograph taken that day in the Manaus studio, of her wearing the kimono and posing beside a huge vase of flowers, found its home on the wall of the Furtado trailer. Enoque Furtado sat back on his bunk to admire it. La Senhora had passed it to him in a moment's embarrassed modesty: 'Because he had expressed a wish for it,' she said, and he had been too overcome with delight to reply. Such a fine figure of a woman! Such a fitting costume for so grand and exotic a lady. The picture took pride of place between his football pennants and his treasure map of Guyana.

So truly, whether or not the kimono ever again saw the light of day, it had already given joy enough to justify its existence. Some things can do that.

GLOSSARY OF PORTUGUESE WORDS

açai: fruit drink

balsa: raft for mining in rivers

bamburrado: someone who has struck lucky

barranco: gully, trench

bateia: pan for mining

brabo: savage

caatinga: area of stunted forest in N.E. Brazil

cachaça: raw spirit from sugar cane

caixa: box, crate

cantina: canteen

carnaval: carnival

chaga: disease-carrying beetle

chope: draught beer

chupadeira: motorized suction pump for mining

churrascaria: barbecue restaurant

cuia: cup, gourd

curupira: bogeyman

desbravador: pioneer pros-pector, hero of a gold strike

despachante: agent, messenger

diarista: daily worker

dono: owner, small scale investor

empada: pasty

fofoca: rumour

forró: free, noisy dance

garimpeiro: miner

garimpo: goldfield

gaucho, carioca, caboclo: people from various parts of Brazil

lanchonete: snack bar

mergulhador: diver

moinho: mill, crusher

mulato: half-caste

paisano: peasant, countryman

peão: worker, farm hand

pium: buffalo gnat

quebrado: out of order

rebaixamento: deepening of a barranco

shaman: Indian magic man

suco: juice

teco-teco: small aeroplane or helicopter

urucu: fruit of annatto tree

Also by Geraldine McCaughrean

A PACK OF LIES

Ailsa doesn't usually pick up men in public libraries — but then M.C.C. Berkshire is rather out of the ordinary and has a certain irresistible charm. Once inside Ailsa and her mother's antiques shop, he also reveals an amazing talent for holding customers spellbound with his extravagant stories — and selling antiques into the bargain!

'Sparkling with wit and originality' – *Guardian*

A LITTLE LOWER THAN THE ANGELS

God, the Devil, Heaven and Hell all stand before Gabriel's eyes. He can scarcely believe them. But when he is forced to flee from his cruel master, the stone mason, and leaps into the red, smoking jaws of Hell, he discovers a whole new and exciting life. But will his new life with the travelling mystery players be any more secure than his old one? In a world of illusions people are not always what they seem. Least of all Gabriel.

DODGEM
Bernard Ashley

Cooped up in council care, Simon and Rose plan a daring escape.

Life hasn't been easy for Simon Leighton. Since the death of his mother, he has had to cope with a depressed father. Afraid to leave him on his own for too long, Simon plays truant from school to look after him. But this eventually lands Simon in council care and his father in hospital.

In the home Simon develops a grudging relationship with a tough young girl called Rose and together they hatch a daring scheme which takes them on an escape route through run-down city streets to the noisy, bustling world of the fairground.

LET THE CIRCLE BE UNBROKEN
Mildred D. Taylor

Maybe it was the way of life to change, but if I had my way I would put an iron padlock on time so nothing would ever have to change again.

For Cassie Logan, 1935 in the American Deep South is a time of bewildering change: the Depression is tightening its grip, rich and poor are in conflict and racial tension is increasing. As she grows away from the security of childhood, Cassie struggles to understand the turmoil around her and the reasons for the deep-rooted fears of her family and friends.

THE ENDLESS STEPPE
Esther Hautzig

Esther Rudomin was ten years old when, in 1941, she and her family were arrested by the Russians and transported to Siberia.

This is the true story of the next five years spent in exile, of how the Rudomins kept their courage high, though they went barefoot and hungry. A magnificent and moving book which will live long in the memory of any reader.

TULKU
Peter Dickinson

Attack in the dark, screams, blazing huts . . .

The Boxer Rebellion reaches a once peaceful mission settlement in remote China. Theodore escapes, and after enduring great danger is drawn to a destiny beyond his imagining – in the mysterious gold-domed monastery of Dong Pe, high in the Tibetan mountains.